Homeward
the Seeking Heart

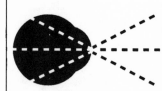

Homeward
the Seeking Heart

JANE PEART

Thorndike Press • **Thorndike, Maine**

Published in 2000 by arrangement with
Baker Book House Company

Scripture quotations in this volume are from the King James
Version of the Bible.

Thorndike Press Large Print Christian Fiction Series.

The tree indicium is a trademark of Thorndike Press.

The text of this Large Print edition is unabridged.
Other aspects of the book may vary from the original edition.

Set in 16 pt. Plantin by Al Chase.

Printed in the United States on permanent paper.

Library of Congress Cataloging-in-Publication Data
Peart, Jane.
    Homeward the seeking heart / Jane Peart.
     p.   cm.
    ISBN 0-7862-2531-9 (lg. print : hc : alk. paper)
    1. Orphan trains — Fiction. 2. Women pioneers —
Fiction. 3. Female friendship — Fiction. 4. Large type
books. I. Title.
PS3566.E238 H66 2000
813'.66—dc21   00-024260

To the *real* "riders" of the orphan trains, the over 100,000 children who were transported by train across the country to new homes in the Mid-west, from 1854 to the early twentieth century, whose experience and courage inspired this series.

1

November 1888

The child stirred and moved restlessly on the makeshift bed, the worn velvet theatrical cloak thrown over her for a blanket slipping to the floor. The sound of loud music — the lively, foot-tapping finale of the music hall's evening's performance — vibrated through the open transom of the shabby dressing room.

With the rolling fanfare of the timpani, the last note merged with enthusiastic applause and echoed down the drafty hallway, soon followed by the sound of high heels clattering on bare boards as the chorus dancers came off stage. A minute later two young women pushed through the door.

"Well, that's it for tonight!" one announced breathlessly.

"My feet are killin' me!" sighed the other, a flashy blond, plopping down into one of two straight chairs before the spotted mirror and kicking off her red satin shoes.

"Shh, Mazel! You'll wake the kid!" cautioned the other dancer, jerking one thumb toward the sleeping child.

"Who, Toddy? Oh, she sleeps right through. She's used to it. Ought to be by now. I've been bringin' her to the theater every night on this run."

"Nobody to leave her with then?"

"Not without payin' a pretty penny. A penny, I might add, that I haven't got. It's all I can do to keep us alive, much less handin' out more for someone to watch her sleep!"

"Don't her father send anything?"

"Who? Him? Johnny Todd? Not on your sweet life, he don't," snapped Mazel with a toss of the brassy blond curls. "I'm not even sure where he is right now, to tell the truth. The last I heard he was with a troupe in Cincinnati."

"So, what are you goin' to do with her if we go on tour with this show?"

Mazel unscrewed the top of a big jar of cold cream and began smearing it over her boldly pretty face, now twisted in a sullen expression.

"Don't know. I haven't got that far with my thinkin', Flo." She spun around and faced her friend. "It's a chance of a lifetime, you know, and I'd hate to miss it. You heard what Barney said. We'd be 'playin' before the crowned heads of Europe' was his exact words."

"Well, you can't drag a little kid all over them foreign places, can you? I mean, you just can't tell what it'll be like" — Flo walked over to where the little girl lay and stood looking down at her. The long-lashed eyelids fluttered slightly. One small plump hand tucked itself under her chin; tangled golden ringlets spread against a tattered pillow.

"You don't need to tell *me* that!" Mazel retorted.

Flo reached down and gently touched a curl, then bent and absentmindedly re-trieved the velvet cloak and tucked it around the sleeping child.

"How old is she anyway?"

"Five goin' on six come next June —"

"Well, what *are* you goin' to do?"

"I've thought of sendin' word to Johnny. Let him face up to his responsibilities for a change. She's his kid, too, after all."

"But if you don't know where he is —" Flo's voice trailed away questioningly.

"I've got his last address. They could forward a letter to him wherever he is now." Mazel shrugged.

"But that might take weeks and Barney said —"

"I *know* what Barney said, Flo. I got ears! We have to let him know by the end of the week if we're goin' on the tour!"

"You couldn't possibly hear from Johnny by then —"

There was a long silence while Mazel removed her heavy stage makeup with a cloth, then flung the cloth down impatiently. She looked at Flo's reflection in the smeared mirror.

"There's always the County Children's Home. I could leave her there, and Johnny could come and get her."

Flo gasped. "You wouldn't!"

"Why not? Ain't that's what we pay taxes for? To support that and the home for old people? That's what it's for, ain't it? For old people and kids who don't have any family —"

"But *she* has parents — you and Johnny. That place is for *orphans,* or kids that are left on the street — *abandoned! You wouldn't, you couldn't leave Toddy there, could you?*"

"Give me another idea then?" Mazel's tone was sarcastic.

Flo looked down again at the little girl, slumbering peacefully, her breath soft and even, unaware that her fate was being decided.

"It would only be *temporary,*" Mazel said slowly as if the idea was catching hold more firmly.

"Temporary?" echoed Flo.

"I already made some inquiries. Under certain circumstances a child can be placed there *temporarily* if there's a family emergency or something that makes it impossible for the parent to keep the child. *Temporarily.*" Mazel kept repeating the word as though it confirmed something. "There's what they call a six-month-period *temporary* placement — that is, if it's a case of necessity —"

"No chance of them, say, puttin' her out for adoption would there be? I mean, in case your letter to Johnny got delayed or somethin', and he didn't come right away to get her?"

"Of course not. You sign papers and that sort of thing. Makes it all legal that it's just *temporary.*"

Flo raised her eyebrows.

"If she was mine, don't think I'd take the chance. She's cute as a button, bright as brass. Somebody might just come along and think, 'I'll take this one home with me.' "

"Oh, for pity's sake, Flo. It ain't like a bakery where you go in and say 'I'll take the cherry tart or the chocolate eclair,' just because it strikes your fancy!" Mazel stood up and turned back and began taking off the red sateen costume with its tarnished gilt-

11

trimmed ruffles. "Come on, hurry up and change! I'm starvin'! Let's go get somethin' to eat."

Flo took her blouse and skirt from the hook that served as a clothes closet, and began to get dressed. Neither woman said anything more until they were both ready to leave.

"What about Toddy?" Flo asked.

"We'll bundle her up and take her back to my room, then we'll go."

"Leave her there alone, do you?"

"My stars, Flo, you're a regular old fuss-budget, ain't you? I'll lock the door. She'll be perfectly safe. I do it all the time. Toddy's sound asleep. She'll never know I'm gone."

2

"Now, sit up straight and stop wigglin'," Mazel ordered as she dragged the brush through Toddy's mass of curls.

Toddy held on to the sides of the chair on which she was sitting and tried not to squirm, squeezing her eyes shut tightly as the brush caught in a tangle. She realized her mother was in no mood to be patient. Especially not after her argument with Flo the night before.

Not that the argument itself had been so unusual. She and Flo often had squabbles sharing the same dressing room. Arguments over costumes, face cream, or kohl, borrowing powder without asking — things like that happened all the time. But this time had been different. This time the argument had been over Toddy.

Having grown up among adults, Toddy had learned early in life to make herself scarce during grown-up conversations. That way she sometimes learned interesting things, although most of the time these discussions were mysteriously beyond her comprehension. Still, she had discovered that the best way to learn anything was to pretend to be playing with her rag doll, the one the costume seamstress had sewn for her, or to stick her nose in a book. In case anyone happened to notice her and remark, "Careful, little pitchers have big ears," she would appear to be preoccupied.

This particular argument had been going on between her mother and Flo for at least a week. Although most of the time it was conducted in lowered voices, last night at the theater, it had exploded.

"What do you know about the place?" Flo had asked Mazel. "I mean you haven't even gone to look at it, see what it's like. Don't you think it's kinda risky?"

"What's risky about it? A roof over her head, three squares a day, a bed to sleep in and other kids to play with — sounds like heaven to me after the way I was dragged around from pillar to post with my folks!" retorted Mazel, slamming down the pot of rouge and unscrewing the lid of the cold cream jar.

"Are you sure Barney won't let you take her along with us?"

At this Mazel spun around, hands on her hips. "I don't *want* to take her along! Can you get that, Flo? This is the chance I've been waitin' for all my life. I mean to take advantage of it and I can't do that with a kid hangin' around my neck every step of the way."

"Well, *excuse me!*" Flo flung back sarcastically. "I'm just saying if she was mine, I couldn't go off to Europe and dump her in some orphanage!"

"Well, she *ain't* your kid, so mind your own business!"

Dead silence followed this exchange in the dressing room that was usually filled with cheerful chatter, joking banter and laughter. Toddy, sitting in the corner tying her doll's yarn hair with a piece of faded ribbon, hummed under her breath and wondered what an "orphanage" was. From under her long lashes she observed her mother, face flashed under the stage makeup, her lips compressed in a straight line.

Pretty soon the caller rapped at the dressing room door, yelling, "On stage, dancers. Cue two minutes." Flo and Mazel, still not speaking, hurried out.

Toddy heard the laughter that followed the exit of the comedian-juggler off stage and the music for the chorus's next set begin. She settled herself on the bench piled with pillows, cushioned by an old folded stage curtain, then hugging her doll, and

15

drawing her favorite costume cast-off, a velvet cape, over her, she curled up and closed her eyes for sleep.

Toddy was accustomed to being left alone in theater dressing rooms. She had been carried into one in a wicker basket less than two weeks after her birth. Her lullabyes had been the tinny sound of a vaudeville band. Old playbills and theater posters had been her first books and pictures. She was "at home" in the backstage of a theater as other children were in a cozy nursery.

It was late when her mother, her face pale, with all greasepaint removed, appeared, bending over her and shaking her. "Wake up, Toddy! It's time to leave! Come on! Get up. You're too big for me to carry you anymore."

Sleepily Toddy roused herself and trudged after Mazel as they walked the deserted midnight streets back to the nearby boardinghouse. Usually Flo walked with them, the two young women laughing and chatting, complaining about the manager, Barney, or swapping gossip about other performers. But this night Flo must have left earlier and her mother seemed grimly silent and preoccupied the whole way. Angry. Toddy could always tell and as soon as they reached their room, she warily undressed

16

and slipped right into the sagging brass bed.

From this vantage point, Toddy watched as Mazel, muttering to herself in some invisible dialogue, began packing. Finally, Toddy's eyes grew heavy and she fell asleep while Mazel was still doggedly making trips back and forth between bureau and trunk.

Early the next morning Mazel awakened Toddy, hurried her through a scanty breakfast of bread and jam and tea, then told her to get dressed. When that wasn't accomplished quickly enough to suit her, Mazel began helping, impatiently jerking arms into sleeves, shoving Toddy's feet into her shoes then struggling with the buttonhook to fasten them. She held out Toddy's coat for her, then jammed on her bonnet and tied the strings.

"Here, take this," she said, handing Toddy her small valise. Rushing to the door, she opened it and called over her shoulder, "Hurry up, we haven't got all day. I've got to meet the others at the train station at ten-thirty and we've got a long way to go before that."

With Mazel pulling Toddy along, they got to the trolley stop just as the streetcar rounded the bend. They climbed the high step up into the car and Mazel bought their tickets, asking the conductor to let her know the closest stop to "Greystone." Then they found seats in the nearly empty car. Toddy enjoyed the rocking motion as the car seemed to careen along the tracks, the bell jangling merrily into the morning air. When it jerked to a sudden stop, the conductor turned to look back at them. "Here's where you want to get off, lady!"

Stepping down from the trolley, they saw they were at the bottom of a steep hill. Mazel sighed heavily.

"Come on," she said and, tugging Toddy by the hand, they started up.

They were both breathless when they reached the top and stood in front of a large, stone building. Toddy looked at her mother curiously, wondering what kind of new adventure the two of them were about to embark on.

Mazel straightened her beribboned hat and adjusted her feather boa before ringing the doorbell. She glanced down at Toddy, then leaned over and, retying her bonnet strings, said brightly, "You're goin' to like it here, Toddy, you'll see."

Toddy ran a finger under her chin, loosening the too tightly tied ribbons a little and just nodded.

A few minutes later they were standing in a high-ceilinged room, opposite a severe looking woman seated behind a huge desk. She had introduced herself as Miss Clinock, head matron of Greystone, and was regarding both of them with a frown.

Much to Toddy's astonishment, her mother began to weep into her handkerchief.

"I have nowhere and no one else to turn to and no other way to support the two of us. We are absolutely alone in the world," she said between sniffles. "There's nothing I want more than to be able to make a home for my little girl. Something I can't do now. With the money I'll be paid on this tour, when I come back I'll —" she stopped and blew her nose. Then shaking her head sorrowfully, she continued, "But until then —"

"Yes, well, Mrs. Todd —" Miss Clinock interrupted, clearing her throat — "just so you fully understand the conditions under which we will accept your daughter." She passed Mazel a sheaf of papers. "Please read these over carefully before you sign them."

The room was very quiet for a few minutes; the only sound was the loud ticking of the wall clock, the tapping of Miss Clinock's own pen on the surface of the desk, and the rustle of papers turning as Mazel skimmed them. Then she stood up, placed them on the desk, and signed her name with a flourish. Miss Clinock took the papers and glanced over them.

"This seems to be in order. Except —" She looked up and the eyebrows over the pince nez rose inquiringly. "You have no address for the father? In case — ?"

"No, ma'am, there's been no word from him in . . . well, in a long time . . . years, in fact."

"All right, Mrs. Todd, you can say goodbye to your daughter now, then we will see that she is taken up to her dormitory and settled in."

Mazel turned to Toddy, bent down, and gave her an impulsive hug. "Now, Toddy, you do as you're told and be a good girl. I'll bring you something nice back from Europe when I come, maybe a big French doll with real hair. You'd like that, wouldn't you?"

For a moment the two of them looked into each other's eyes — Toddy's innocent but puzzled, Mazel's now amazingly dry. Then Mazel blinked and turned quickly away. What Toddy saw in her mother's eyes she could not name but instinctively recognized. It was abandonment.

3

Greystone Orphanage

Toddy sat on the edge of the narrow bed, assessing her new situation. Her feet, now encased in itchy black woolen stockings and shod in sturdy black shoes that laced to the ankles, swung back and forth. She smoothed down the front of the blue muslin pinafore buttoned over a coarse cotton dress. Then she turned up the hem and examined the untrimmed flannel petticoat and biscuit-colored pantaloons. She had been given these in exchange for the clothes in which she had arrived. Those had all been removed by Miss Doby, the matron in charge of Greystone uniform and supplies, with a look of obvious disapproval.

Toddy gave a sigh of resignation. She had always liked the things Mazel paid Tess, the theater costumer, to cut down or make over from her own discarded blouses and skirts into outfits for Toddy. Mazel liked bright colors, patterns and flowered material, lace and ribbon trims, and so did Toddy. But it didn't really matter. She wouldn't be here long.

Toddy looked around the long room with its high windows and the double row of small iron cots. Beside each one was a chest of drawers, on which was set a white enamel washbowl and pitcher. Next to it was an unpainted wooden stool.

So this was the "orphanage" where Flo thought she shouldn't be "dumped."

Toddy was used to sudden moves, abrupt changes in living arrangements. She was not afraid of strangers nor of new places. Her mother had often left her with people she scarcely knew for periods of time varying from overnight to a week or more. Since Toddy had the curiosity of a kitten she enjoyed exploring and experiencing different environments. Her innate sense of adventure enabled her to discover something interesting wherever she found herself.

At her age, Toddy had no real sense of time. Her mother had left her before but always came back. Undoubtedly she would do so this time as well. In the meantime — Toddy gave a little bounce on the mattress but it resisted. She shrugged. It was as easy for Toddy to sleep on the rigid seat of a day coach as on a pile of theatrical costumes or in an empty trunk. She had done all three.

Luckily for her, she could adjust to this set of circumstances as easily as any other.

As she sat there absorbing her new surroundings, she heard the sound of running
feet along the linoleum hall outside, the
muffled sound of children's voices. Then
the dormitory doors burst open and in
rushed a group of girls. They halted at the
sight of Toddy.

A chunky, red-headed girl, taller than the
others, pushed to the front and addressed
her loudly. "Hey you! You're new, ain't
you!" she asked accusingly. "What's your
name?"

Toddy, who always expected to be liked,
smiled and got to her feet. "I'm Toddy!"

The girl walked forward, followed by the
rest trooping behind her. Approaching
Toddy she shoved her fat, freckled face
right up into hers and said belligerently,
"Think you're smart, don't you?"

The others tittered behind hands clapped
to their mouths, eager to see what was going
to happen next.

Toddy wasn't used to being around other
children, but she recognized a bully when
she met one. This girl with her squinty eyes,
jutting chin, and pugnacious manner was
threatening her for some reason. Somehow
Toddy knew that the rest of her days at
Greystone depended on this moment. She
remembered what she'd been taught by the

Carelli Brothers, an Italian acrobatic team who had traveled with the troupe for a season.

"No, I don't think I'm 'specially smart, but I can show you a trick!"

"What kind of a trick?" The girl seemed startled.

"Stand back," Toddy said pleasantly.

The girl backed up a few steps.

With that, Toddy moved from where she was standing beside her cot out into the aisle. She took a deep breath and then executed a series of cartwheels down the length of the room. Over and over she went until she finished the last one and stood up triumphantly. Hearing a unified gasp behind her, she turned around grinning. Immediately a cluster of little girls surrounded her. At that minute Toddy knew she was accepted. She had defeated whatever purpose the pudgy redhead, whose name she was told was Molly B., had intended. And in doing so she had earned the admiration of the others.

Just then they all heard the snap of wooden clappers and Miss Massey, their dormitory matron, stood at the entrance.

"Come girls, time for outdoor recreation. Get your sweaters and form a line to go out to the play yard."

From that time on Toddy's place was established within the pecking order of Greystone Orphanage. She was a born leader with a personality like quicksilver, sparkling and spontaneous. She had a wonderful comedic sense, no doubt inherited from her wandering father, the elusive Johnny Todd, and was an effortless mimic. She could turn any situation into an adventure, delighting and entertaining the other children.

Coming as she did from the drama of the backstage theater world where all was chaos, color and change into this one where order, discipline and routine prevailed was a drastic transition. However it might have been harder for her to fit in so easily had she not comforted herself with the belief that she was only a "temporary" placement.

But as the weeks and months passed, the seed of possibility that her mother might never come back to get her began to take hold. She'd received two postcards dashed off by Mazel — one, a picture of Buckingham Palace in London, "where the Queen lives" scribbled on it, the other, written on the boat train to France. There had been nothing after that. Toddy kept those two cards under her pillow, taking them out, examining them, rereading the brief messages over and over until the edges were worn.

Then one day Molly B. confronted her in the hall.

"Is your *real* name Zephronia Victorine Todd?" she demanded.

One of the first toys Toddy ever got was a set of blocks from Flo who had taught her to spell out her name years ago. This feat had always been a source of pride for Toddy.

She drew herself up and replied, "Yes, it is, why?"

"I'll tell you why, Miss Smarty. I saw your name on the list in Miss Clinock's office. You've been transferred from 'temporary' to 'permanent'. That means you're just like all the rest of us now. *An orphan, no mother, no father, no home!*" With this Molly B. stuck out her tongue and made an awful face. Then, laughing maliciously, she ran off down the hall.

Toddy stood looking after her. A cold chill, like an icy finger, trailed down her spine. Up until now Toddy had held on to the hope that Mazel *would* show up with the big French doll and they would go "home" together to whatever shoddy boardinghouse that might be.

No one else had witnessed the scene between the two girls in the deserted hall, and Toddy told no one about it. Whatever Toddy felt she buried deep inside, and showed no visible distress. It was all hidden behind the smile, the twinkling eyes, the ready wit. Popular with the orphans and staff alike, Toddy seemed carefree and reasonably happy.

But Toddy had no real friend at Greystone until Kit Ternan arrived.

Kit was the quietest person Toddy had ever known. One day Miss Massey brought her to the classroom, and the teacher assigned her to sit with Toddy. She slipped in beside Toddy on the other side of the double school desk Toddy occupied. Toddy smiled at her new seatmate and the smile was shyly returned. Kit had shiny brown hair, neatly parted and braided into two long plaits, and large, clear gray eyes. They shared a reader and a slate to do sums until Kit was given her own supplies. When the recess bell rang, Toddy took Kit in tow, escorting her to the long tables where they picked up their mid-morning "tea" of a slice of buttered bread and a mug of watery cocoa.

Little by little Toddy's warmth and friendliness overcame Kit's initial reticence and the two became inseparable. Kit was given the cot next to Toddy's in the dormitory and after the "lights out" bell, the two whispered confidences. Toddy found out

Kit had a little brother and sister who were in the Primary and Nursery sections of Greystone, and that she would be allowed to visit them on Sundays.

"But that's not often enough!" Kit mourned, wiping the tears that kept rolling out of her beautiful eyes. "I've always taken care of Gwynny. She's not used to anyone else, and I *know* she misses me terribly. And Jamie is shy. I'm worried about how he'll be getting along with other boys, 'specially if they're rough and all."

Toddy tried to comfort Kit, but not ever having had any brothers and sisters of her own, she did not really understand. Still, her sympathetic heart and natural instincts helped more than she was aware. After a few Sunday visits Kit seemed somewhat reassured that Gwynny was well cared for and Jamie was getting along surprisingly well.

Toddy lost track of the months she had been at Greystone when the other child who would become her friend and the third member of the little trio that would be jestingly referred to by the staff as "the Three Musketeers" arrived at Greystone.

Laurel Vestal caused quite a sensation among the girls in the dormitory. She looked like the French doll Toddy imagined her mother might have brought her on her return from Paris. She had rosy cheeks, round brown eyes, and dark curls that tumbled over her shoulders and reached her waist in back. She was dressed in a blue velour coat with a short scalloped cape and a matching bonnet she refused to take off. She sat, with her arms crossed determinedly, on the little stool beside her cot, her mouth trembling and tears hovering brightly in her dark eyes.

The other orphans were all watching to see how the matrons were going to deal with this dilemma. Toddy and Kit were especially anxious because the new girl's cot had been placed between their two. They could hear her sobbing at night and longed to do something. As if by mutual agreement, the third night they both crept out of their own beds and, sitting on either side of Laurel, one held her hand, while the other gently stroked her hair away from her hot, tear-wet face.

Eventually, by what means the children never knew, Laurel dressed in the Greystone uniform, entered the classroom, and took a desk not far from Toddy and Kit. At the bell for recess, both girls ran over to Laurel, took her hands, and led her out to the recreation yard.

From then on an unspoken bond was forged between the three, one that would develop into a friendship to last all their lives.

4

Meadowridge

The face of the young man leaning forward from the pulpit of Meadowridge Community Church was earnest. His eyes searched the congregation for the response he sought.

"Picture, if you will, young boys, many eight years old and younger, huddled in doorways, their clothes ragged, their feet shoeless in the freezing cold of a New England winter — or a squalid tenement flat where a sick mother lies in bed covered by a threadbare blanket while her children hover around a cold stove, hungry and bewildered by the circumstances over which they have no control. Consider the plight of three pitiful youngsters shivering in a doorway of a large industrial city abandoned by an alcoholic father —"

Matthew Scott, only recently ordained as a minister, halted and looked into the faces of the assembly of well-fed, well-dressed citizens of Meadowridge. How could they possibly understand what he was trying to convey? "God help me," he prayed silently before going on.

"If this brings a twinge of compassion or a wince of distaste or, hopefully, an urge to help alleviate some of the suffering I have described, then I plead with you now to consider what I am going to propose. The Rescuers and Providers Society, which I represent, has done a mighty work in taking some of these children off the streets and finding homes for them among the warm-hearted people of the West. In the generous heartland of our great country, we have found willing families to welcome these helpless children into their loving care, giving them the affection and protection, every child's birthright, of which cruel fate has robbed them.

"In the five years the Society has been actively involved in rescuing these children, providing for them, outfitting them, sending them by train into rural communities throughout the western United States, we have hundreds of stories of children whose lives have been changed, families who have been blessed by their presence.

"I have spent two days in your beautiful town and the surrounding countryside. I have walked your shady streets, looked at your pleasant houses, well-kept yards, observed the faces of the people I have encountered. I have driven beyond the township limits into the rural areas, admired the rolling pastures with sleek cattle grazing, sheep on the hillsides, the white-washed fences, brightly painted barns, flourishing vegetable gardens and neat farmhouses. Everywhere I have seen evidence of prosperity, contentment, absorbed the healthy wholesome atmosphere, the perfect environment for any fortunate child."

Here Matthew paused, bowed his head, as if he found it difficult to continue. Then, his voice husky with emotion, he went on.

"When I remember the places I have visited in the city — the shacks, the tenement houses, the bleak institutions where dozens of children wait in vain to be adopted — and see the great contrast to life here, I am overwhelmed. But because of it, I am encouraged, yes, bold enough to ask you who live in these bountiful circumstances — will you share what you have been given with others so much less fortunate? Will you take a child — perhaps you have room even for two children — into your homes, to raise in this healthy, Christian atmosphere? If you can find it in your heart to make such a commitment, I can guarantee that *you* will be beneficiary as well as benefactor. God's

33

generosity can never be surpassed.

"If any of you who have been moved by the testimonies I have recounted and feel led to offer your home to one of these hapless little ones, my wife, Anna, and I will be here — the guests of your pastor's kind hospitality — for the next few days. If you want more information, if you want to talk further with us about any aspect of such an adoption, we will be more than happy to answer all your questions.

"In closing, it is my sincere prayer that next spring when Anna and I are accompanying these children west, one of our stops will be in Meadowridge. Thank you and God bless you all."

After church, Mrs. Olivia Hale came into her house, the enormous Victorian some people in Meadowridge considered magnificent and others called a monstrosity. With its three tiers of balconies, overhanging eaves, elaborate fretwork under the peaked roof, it loomed over the town from its hilltop like a claret-colored giant.

She paused briefly before the hall mirror to remove her hat with its crepe mourning veil and to smooth her hair, untouched by more than a trace of gray. Olivia was a tall, handsome woman in her mid-fifties, dressed in a black faille dress, a black onyx brooch at its high collar, fluted ruching at the wrist of its long "leg-of-mutton" sleeves. Although she had been a widow for more than twenty years, Olivia had never put aside the traditional black. She continued to wear "widow's weeds" more out of habit and lack of interest in fashion than any morbid clinging to the past. Olivia was too strong-minded to live in the past. It was the very real present which concerned her this morning.

She remained standing there a few minutes, not to view her reflection, but because she was preoccupied with her own thoughts. The appeal made by the visiting minister this morning had been very moving, had touched a deep responding chord in Olivia's heart. But it was something she wanted to consider very carefully before she took any action.

As if agreeing with this wise decision, the woman in the glass gave an imperceptible nod of her head. The rather stern expression seemed to soften momentarily as Olivia smiled to herself, turned and went into the parlor.

Moving with the erect carriage of someone much younger, she seated herself in a sculptured mahogany armchair in the bay window. From this vantage point she looked down upon the town and the river beyond. It was because of this fine view that her late husband, Ed, had chosen this spot as the site of the mansion he wanted built soon after he struck it rich in the gold fields and they moved to Meadowridge.

At the thought of Ed, Olivia automatically turned to look at the elaborate gold-framed portrait over the black marble fireplace.

Olivia sighed. Even after all these years, she still missed the towering, raw-boned fellow with his thundering voice, his glass-shattering laugh, his insistence on wearing cowboy boots with the $400 suits he had tailored for himself in San Francisco. Granted, as the years went on, they were hand-tooled Moroccan leather ones, but none the less he must have felt the boots kept him in touch with the "old days."

Olivia smoothed the silky ribbed fabric of her skirt with one ring-encrusted hand. After all the years of following her husband from mining camp to mining camp, Ed had showered her with every luxury once he had made his fortune. He liked the showy kind, such as the huge canary diamond solitaire she wore next to the thin gold band he had placed on her finger when she had married him at sixteen. Beneath a brusque exterior, Olivia was sentimental, and she would never let Ed replace that cheap little wedding ring. Instead, he gave her more rings, brooches, pendants, earrings.

Yes, she missed him *and* their only son, Richard. Left fatherless as a ten-year-old boy, Dick had grown up with the legend of Big Ed and had spent his life trying to live up to his father's reputation, though he was nothing like him in physical build or temperament. Dick was killed breaking a new horse, thrown as he was trying to prove he was every bit the man his father had been. And right before the eyes of his fragile, young wife, Marilee.

Olivia winced as if warding off the shock of it again, as if it had happened just yesterday instead of seven years ago. Marilee had not lived long after Dick's fatal accident. Died of a broken heart, many said. Olivia did not agree. No one died of a broken heart. If so, *she* would have been dead long since. Instead, Olivia had gone on living, bringing up the delicate little girl her son and his wife had left — Helene, her adored granddaughter.

This should have made up for all the heartbreak Olivia had suffered, but there was yet another blow to be borne. It was discovered Helene had a defective heart. Ever since, Olivia had lived from day to day with the threat of losing her, too.

Although Helene was now nearly twelve, she had never been able to attend school or lead a normal child's life. Though Olivia was able to afford tutors, a nurse to care for her, it was not enough. Helene was lonely for companionship, children her own age. The problem was, no normally active child would be content to sit quietly and play lap games, or do watercolors, or read, the way Helene's precarious health required.

Again, Olivia's eyes turned to the lantern jawed man in the oil painting, whose keen blue eyes seemed to regard her with a mixture of ironic humor and shrewd wisdom. Often in times of indecision or anxiety, Olivia found herself turning to that picture of Ed, whom the artist's masterly skill had brought so vividly to life, as if seeking in some ways the advice she had always sought from him when he was alive.

The words of the young man who had spoken at church that morning echoed in Olivia's mind.

"We plan to bring a specified number of children ranging in ages from five to ten by train next spring, making stops at the towns where folk have agreed to take these children into their homes, adopt them as their own.

"I would remind you of Christ's own admonition: 'Whoever does this to the least of these, will have done it unto me.' "

Olivia had never considered herself particularly spiritual. Oh, she was God fearing and churchgoing, but she had always been a down-to-earth, sensible sort of person. That is why what happened to her as she listened to this earnest young man's appeal was so startling. Quite unexpectedly she had felt a stinging sensation behind her eyes and a definite sharp twinge in the region of her heart. It was almost as if the Lord Himself were saying, "Here is your answer. You have room in your house and your heart for another child — a companion for Helene."

Olivia had felt quite uncomfortable. She had glanced quickly around her to see if anyone sitting near her had noticed anything strange or heard anything. But of course, she knew it was an inner voice. A gentle nudging within, a thought quietly planted but not easily dismissed. She was not given to emotional reactions or sudden demonstrations of religious zeal. However, on the way home in her elegant carriage after the church service, she realized her experience did not fade. In fact the thought grew stronger that this was something she should do.

And if I brought a child to live here — and it would have to be a girl — she would have to be a very special type, one who could adapt herself to a household centered on a young invalid. Would I be able to find such a child among those on the Orphan Train that young man and his wife are bringing out here next spring?

Some of those he described were street urchins. He had told heartrending stories of such children. No, it would never do to have a child with that kind of background come to live with Helene here. Of course, Mr. Scott explained, not all the children had been abandoned, left to live by their wits on city streets. Some were the victims of homes ravaged by incurable illness, death, or desertion by one parent. Many were from "homes such as your own," he had pointed out, where death or disaster of one kind or another had struck.

Scott and his wife were staying at Reverend Brewster's house while they were in Meadowridge. For the next few days they would be interviewing prospective adopting families, he said.

Gradually Olivia's thoughts took shape. She would write a note, outlining her requirements for a child suitable to be Helene's companion — the personality, age, interests that would be necessary in order for her to fit into this household.

Yes, she would do that right away, then arrange to have Mr. Scott and his wife come to tea. Meeting Helene would give them a better idea of what kind of child to place with her.

Having made the decision, Olivia immediately rose, went straight to her desk, took out her fine stationery with the swirled gold monogram at the top, and, dipping her pen into the inkwell, began to write.

5

Greystone Orphanage
March 1890

Anna Scott controlled a shudder as she and her husband, Matthew, approached the tall, forbidding building behind the black iron-spoked fence. The afternoon was gray, the sky heavy with dark clouds. A fierce wind tossed the barren branches of the few trees. Even though it was the last week in March, there was not a sign of spring anywhere — not a crocus, or a green bud, or a robin to give hope of its coming.

Anna took Matthew's arm with one hand as they mounted the stone steps; with the other, she held onto her bonnet while her cloak billowed behind her like a sail. Maybe the bleakness of the day had something to do with her odd feeling of depression, Anna told herself.

As they waited for an answer to the door-bell, Anna gazed at her husband adoringly. Their first year of marriage, filled as it had been with difficulties, almost constant traveling, strange towns, new experiences,

coping with the obstacles and discourage-
ment, had nonetheless been a fulfilling one.
Their love had remained as steadfast as
Matthew's determination to achieve his inspired vision.

Since the day he had come to her church
and spoken of his dream to take every
homeless child, abandoned or orphaned, to
a Christian home in the rural heartland of
the country, Anna had been unwavering in
her admiration, respect and devotion for
Matthew.

She still considered him the most ideal of
all possible choices she might have made in
a husband, and herself the most fortunate of
women that he eventually returned her love
and asked her to join him in his quest.

Anna knew she fell far short of the paragon such a man was entitled to in a wife,
but she prayed every day to be more worthy.

His high-mindedness, lofty morals, and
idealistic goals had drawn her to him with
blinding fervor. Now, as all his hopes and
ideals were at last coming to fruition, she
stood beside him with strong confidence in
his ability as he stood firm in the faith that
he was doing God-ordained work.

It was her own competence she doubted,
her own capabilities that seemed inadequate for the task before them.

Greystone Orphanage was the last institution they were contacting to fill the quota of children they would be escorting west. Matthew had spoken at a dozen churches in these communities willing to receive these orphans.

Anna came from a sheltered home where she had grown up an only child. She had no real experience caring for children. She had attempted teaching a Sunday school once. But with no gift for keeping a room full of lively eight- to ten-year-old boys and girls in order, she had quickly resigned as a volunteer teacher.

How on earth would she manage overseeing a train carload of orphans across the country on the transcontinental railroad? She had asked herself often, with inner trepidation. She would repeat the Scripture verse from Philippians that Matthew was fond of quoting to her whenever she expressed her doubts: "I can do all things through Christ which strengtheneth me."

Just then Matthew turned and smiled at her encouragingly as though he had been reading her thoughts. Anna smiled back, although her lips trembled a little. Then the door was opened by a gaunt-looking woman and Matthew introduced them, saying they had an appointment with Greystone's Head

Matron, Miss Clinock.

The woman nodded. "I'm Miss Massey, Miss Clinock's assistant. She's expecting you. If you'll wait here in the hall, I'll tell her you've come."

As she stepped across the threshold into the shadowy hallway, another quotation flashed through Anna's mind: "All hope abandon, ye who enter here." Where had *that* come from? And why should she think of it now?

As they stood waiting they heard the tramp of dozens of little boots and Anna turned in the direction from which the sound came. Two lines of little girls were descending the wide main staircase.

When they reached the bottom, the matron in charge herded them into a single line, straightening the line with little pushes and shoves as she walked its length.

To a less sensitive, observant person than Anna, they might have all looked alike, dressed as they were in identical buff cotton dresses, blue denim pinafores, black stockings, and black high-top shoes. But for some reason, Anna's eyes were drawn to one child who was returning her look with curiosity and interest.

She had a gamin face with round blue eyes sparkling with mischief, and a turned-up nose. Dimples winked on either side of a rosy mouth. Riotous red-gold curls had escaped the tight braids into which someone had attempted to confine her hair.

There was something immensely appealing about this little girl that evoked an immediate response in Anna. Then she noticed the child directly behind her. She had an enchanting beauty that the drab institutional outfit did nothing to diminish. A cameo perfection in miniature, a Dresden doll with rosy porcelain cheeks, dark eyes, wavy dark hair that also defied the restraint of plaits.

She seemed to be daydreaming and had absentmindedly stepped out of line as the matron was passing. The woman halted and said something in a sharp tone, then took her by the shoulder and jerked her back into formation.

Anna was indignant. That was unnecessary, she thought. But even as she watched, she saw another little girl, taller, slimmer. Her shiny brown hair was neatly parted, correctly braided. She remained quietly waiting in line, not wiggling or looking around as the little impish one was doing, nor lost in her own thoughts like the other one. As Anna watched she saw her slip her hand over and pat the shoulder of the child who had been reprimanded. Then the two exchanged a smile.

Something warm seemed to coat Anna's heart at this small unnoticed act of comfort and kindness. Her interest at once focused on the comforter. For some reason these three children seemed to stand out from the rest.

As if sensing Anna's gaze, the child returned her look. Anna drew in her breath, stunned by the sweetness of expression and most of all by the child's beautiful eyes. At that moment the matron snapped her wooden clapper and the line of children began to move forward.

Anna let out her breath slowly. Even though it had lasted a mere second, something indefinable had passed between her and that sad-eyed little girl. Anna was moved to her very depths. For the first time in this entire year of talking about them, searching for homes for them, she realized that the "orphans" who were Matthew's cause, his life's purpose, and through him, now hers, were more than that — they were individuals, each different, separate, with hearts and minds and souls of their own.

Each of those little girls with whom she had had the briefest kind of encounter had their own history, their own story to tell, their own life to live.

And maybe now she, Anna Maury Scott, could be part of it. Maybe in some small way she could help them find the home they needed, the home that would nourish them, love them —

"Miss Clinock will see you now. Come in, please." Miss Massey's voice snapped Anna back to the present.

Gripped by the impact of her new insight, Anna took a seat beside Matthew in the austere office of Greystone's Head Matron. She listened as Matthew discussed the requirements for orphans to be taken on the Orphan Train.

"They must be in good health, and at least old enough to take care of themselves physically, that is, dressing, hygiene, and the necessities. They must be reasonably intelligent, capable of understanding and appreciating the opportunity they are being given."

"And how many from Greystone will you be able to handle?" Miss Clinock asked, her pen poised over a paper bearing a long list of names.

"On this trip we are limited to fifteen children from each of the four institutions with whom we have made arrangements," Matthew answered.

"Only fifteen?" Miss Clinock tapped her bottom teeth with the tip of her pen and sighed. "And so many children need homes —"

"I know," Matthew agreed with a sorrowful shake of his head. "But our resources are, alas, limited, as well. Only two railroad cars have been allotted to us — one for boys, the other for girls. Contributions to our Society are the main funding for this enterprise and we have to figure food along the way, with a contingency fund in case of any unforeseen events, any sort of emergency." He paused. "We expect to be helped out by the prospective adopting families in the towns where we will be stopping. The churches involved plan to have a kind of Orphan Train Day. They will serve a meal, give the families considering adoption and the children time to meet, get to know each other a little, talk together — talk with us. Then the children who are selected will go home with their new parents and the rest of us will get back on the train and go on to the next designated town."

Miss Clinock nodded. "It seems a sound plan. Then you *do* expect all the children to be adopted?"

"That is our fond hope, our earnest prayer," Matthew replied solemnly.

"As you may now know, Reverend Scott, Greystone is largely for the shelter of very young abandoned and orphaned children. We do not keep children after they enter their teens. At that time boys go to the Poor Boys' Home over in Milltown; most go to work in the cotton mill there until they are eighteen and on their own. The girls we divide into two classes. The brighter ones we try to find apprenticeships for in various trades, the rest go into factory work." Miss Clinock sighed, then continued, "What I'm saying is, our babies are pretty much in demand and do not stay here long. Neither do the temporaries, that is, the children who are placed here during family crises of some sort for a short time, and are usually claimed by relatives even if something has happened to their real parents." Here Miss Clinock paused significantly. "It is the older children, the ones *past* that cunning baby stage so attractive to childless couples, who are hard to place," she said with an ironic half-smile. "You know everyone wants a blue-eyed, blond, curly-headed baby girl."

Miss Clinock rose from her seat behind the desk and paced the narrow room again. "So, I suggest I pick a few of these children for you to meet, and then we can decide who are the best potential travelers to take with you on the Orphan Train." She checked the watch pinned to the lapel of her fitted brown bombazine jacket. "The children are at recreation now. It is a half-hour until their midday meal. This would be a good time to see them when they are unaware that they are being inspected or singled out in any way."

She went to the door, opened it, and motioned them to come with her. As they followed her pencil-slim figure down the corridor, Anna breathed a prayer that the three special little girls would be among the children chosen for her to "shepherd" to their new homes in the West.

6

Orphan Train
En Route

At the far end of the transcontinental railway car that was now converted into a moving dormitory, Anna Scott sat reading her Bible by the wavering light of an oil lamp suspended from the rack over her head.

She was tired and found it difficult to keep her mind from wandering. They had been traveling for three weeks and Anna was feeling both physically spent and emotionally discouraged. She had never imagined the task she had so willingly taken on would prove so wearying, so mentally fatiguing.

Keeping the children occupied from early in the morning when the first one awakened until the last one settled down at night was exhausting. At first she had tried to set up some kind of routine for the day — washing up, short devotions and morning prayers, then passing out the jam and bread and apples that composed their breakfast, this followed by a semblance of some kind of lessons.

Anna had brought along a map of the United States and pinned it to the wall, showing the children where they were each day and pointing out the next stop. She had taught them a number of games to play in groups, and often she would gather them together to sing hymns as well as songs in which there was clapping or some kind of activity. Still, with all her efforts, the days were long.

One welcome diversion was the frequent stops the train made to take on food for the dining car, water, wood and coal. Then Anna would bundle the children off the train and march them along the platform for fresh air and exercise. If the stop was long enough and there was a nearby field, she would encourage a game of tag or run-sheep-run. This helped the children release some of the pent-up energy stifled by their confinement in the train.

Anna had also brought along some books and read aloud to the girls in the evenings before bedtime and evening prayers — prayers that always ended with the sincere cry of her heart, "That each child will find a loving home."

Of the thirty little girls who had accompanied her from Boston, eleven remained, with only two more towns where they were scheduled to stop, towns which had expressed interest in becoming adoptive parents to some of the children on this trainload of orphans.

But if some of these who were left were not adopted, what would she and Matthew do? In some of the towns where the original response and enthusiasm had been high, only a few people had come forward to claim their adopted children. And those mostly boys. Farm families needed extra "hands," Anna realized. But these little girls needed homes, too.

She raised her head, feeling the tension in her neck and shoulders. She had been searching through the Psalms, seeking verses from which she could find renewed encouragement and strength. But now the words on the page had begun to blur. Anna blinked her tired eyes and looked down the length of the darkened car.

At night the backs of seats were turned down and over, pillows and blankets spread upon them and made into beds. Most of the children were sound asleep. Except for the three huddled together in the far corner at the very end. Judging from the muffled sound of their whispers and giggles, *those* three were still awake.

Anna stifled a smile. Maybe she should

get up, go down to them, reprimand them. But, on second thought, what harm were they doing? They didn't seem to be disturbing anyone else.

For a minute, Anna's eyes rested on the three little heads so close together, one a tousled golden mop of ringlets, the next a tangle of dark curls, the third a smooth crown of satiny brown. From the first, Anna was intrigued by this trio. Toddy, Laurel and Kit — such contrasts in every way and yet seemingly inseparable.

Anna frowned unconsciously. It puzzled her that none of the three had yet been adopted. They were certainly among the most winsome of all the girls. Yet at stop after stop, they reboarded the train with the other unselected ones, while some of the less attractive children were chosen right away.

Anna simply couldn't understand why. Just then the murmur of voices grew louder, followed by a peal of light laughter. Anna looked sharply in the direction of this burst of merriment, and knew she must act before they awakened the other children.

She made her way down the aisle between the rows of sleeping bodies, lying in every possible position, until she reached the laughing culprits.

Trying to sound stern, she whispered, "Now, you girls must settle down immediately. You will wake the others up. And tomorrow's a big day. You all need a good night's sleep," she reminded them, tucking their blankets around them.

Returning to her own place at the other end of the car, Anna's questions were still not answered. The sight of each angelic little face lingered in her mind's eye.

These three had everything any adoptive mother could want — personality, alertness, charm. Laurel was so pretty; Toddy, so quick and amusing; Kit with such sweetness, such spontaneous generosity — who would not fall in love with one of them or, for that matter, all three?

She wished she could discuss this dilemma with Matthew. But he was in the other car with the boys and there was no passageway between. Anna sighed. He probably had his hands full with problems of his own, anyway.

During all this journey, she and Matthew had had little chance to exchange more than a few words. They each were so busy with their charges, and at the train stops, dealing with the questions of the prospective parents or the merely curious.

Some of *those* asked the most outrageous

questions! Anna's cheeks burned with indignation at some of the tactless people she had encountered. Some made disparaging remarks about the children right in front of them, commenting on their appearance, their size, as if children had no ears, much less *feelings!*

People said things they would never say about another adult. At least not in their hearing. And these folks were supposed to be Christians! It made Anna so furious she often had to send up a hurried prayer for forgiveness at her thoughts.

As she got ready to make herself as comfortable as possible on her own narrow carseat bed, the same disturbing worry intruded itself. What would they do if some of the children never found a home? What would become of them? Were Matthew and she compelled to return them to the orphanage from which they came? Anna bit her lip. That was one possibility she and her husband had never discussed.

As she plaited her hair, a preview of tomorrow's scene flashed through Anna's mind. If it followed the pattern of the other towns where the Orphan Train had stopped, she knew approximately what to expect.

Looking their very best, hair neat, faces

scrubbed, shoes shined, the children would come off the train and line up on the platform where the townspeople were usually awaiting their arrival.

There was always someone in charge, the minister of the hosting church, or his wife, or some members of the City Council. Matthew was the one who handled that aspect. Anna was too nervous overseeing the children, hoping no one had an urgent need to use the "necessary" or that none of the boys would start shoving or poking each other or pulling a girl's pigtail.

Even for Anna, the inspection ordeal was agonizing. She could only imagine what it must be like for the children being inspected!

She never was sure, except in the case of some of the taller, heftier-looking boys who were taken right away by a sharp-eyed farmer, why one child was chosen over another. But tomorrow, Anna determined, she was going to pay special attention to Toddy, Laurel and Kit. She would try to discern why they had not yet been selected for adoption.

Anna bunched up her pillow, curled herself on the unyielding makeshift mattress, and tried to settle herself for sleep. But sleep did not come easily. Those three little faces kept her awake.

Tomorrow she would try to move about, eavesdrop a little, listen to the comments exchanged between the couples looking over the children, try to see what they discussed among themselves. Perhaps she could figure out the riddle of why, out of all the orphans, Toddy, Laurel and Kit remained unclaimed.

Anna closed her eyes wearily. She knew she had broken all the rules outlined by Reverend Macy, the founder of the Rescuers and Providers Society, at the rally just before the Orphan Train pulled out. The cardinal rule: DO NOT ALLOW YOURSELF TO BECOME EMOTIONALLY INVOLVED WITH THE CHILDREN.

"You are there to administer Christian charity, to follow our Lord's admonition to care for the poor, the widows and orphans of this world. Keep in mind that it is your duty to see that these children are placed in good homes," he told them emphatically.

Well, she had failed, Anna sighed. A persistent idea would not go away. If, for whatever reason, no one adopted those three little girls, she and Matthew could take them! Her own thought surprised her to full wakefulness, maybe because it was the first independent decision she had made in her entire life. She had been a dutiful daughter to her father, and for a little over a year now, a submissive wife to Matthew. How could she possibly be so positive she would make such a life-altering decision without even consulting her husband?

Anna pulled the covers over her suddenly shivering shoulders and shut her eyes determinedly. Before she drifted off, her last conscious thoughts were the words of Scripture from Matthew 6:34: "Take therefore no thought for the morrow, for the morrow shall take thought for the things of itself. Sufficient unto the day is the evil thereof."

In the morning the train chugged into the Springview station, with its engine emitting puffs of steam and the whistle giving a shrill toot. Peering out one of the car windows, Anna saw a crowd of people clustered on the depot platform, craning their necks as the train screeched to a stop and scanning the windows for a glimpse of its cargo.

Anna felt the familiar tightness in her middle, and her palms were damp as she pulled on her gloves. She looked over the children pushing into the aisles, surveying them anxiously.

"Remember be pleasant, polite and above all — smile!" she coached them. "Are we all ready? Come along then," she said, leading the way.

Toddy tugged at both Laurel's and Kit's arms, saying in a stage whisper, "Now, don't forget. Kit, *you* be sure not only to turn your foot sideways, but drag it and *limp!*" Then turning to Laurel, she instructed her, "Remember, hunch up your shoulders, one higher than the other, and twist your mouth. See? Like this." She modeled an awful grimace.

Laurel made an attempt to comply.

Toddy looked doubtful. "Try to stay behind me as though you can't walk right on your own. And I'll — how's this?" she asked, crossing her eyes.

The other two clapped hands over their mouths to suppress their giggles.

"Careful!" Toddy hissed warningly. "This has *got* to work, remember!"

With that, the three fell in at the end of the line of children following the distracted Mrs. Scott out of the train.

For the next half-hour Anna was completely involved in the business at hand, surrounded by inquisitive people with insistent questions.

As soon as they had descended from the train, they were greeted by the Mayor and his wife, who immediately tucked her arm through Anna's and led the way to the Town Hall.

"The church ladies have set out a very nice lunch, brought all their best recipes. We *knew* the poor little dears must be starving," Mrs. McLeod purred. "And *you* must be worn to a frazzle. Some refreshment is what everybody needs. Some food to restore your strength which I'm sure has been sorely tried on this long journey." She patted Anna's arm comfortingly. Not waiting for Anna's disclaimer, she continued, "No matter how good children are — they can be — well, we all know how trying little ones that age can be, don't we, my dear?"

Mrs. McLeod was an indefatigable talker and so Anna did not get in a word all the way on the walk to the Square. At the Town Hall the wives of all the members of the City Council, dressed to the nines for the occasion, were lined up to meet her.

They plied her with cake, coffee and conversation so that she had no chance to keep an eye on the children. But Matthew was there, and she sent up a silent prayer that he had everything under control as she tried to concentrate on what one of the Council ladies was telling her about her sciatica.

At least a half hour passed before a

woman, who had been circling and hovering during her chats with some of the other ladies, finally cornered her. Blocking access to anyone else, she planted herself firmly in front of Anna.

Skewering Anna with a cold, stilettolike gaze she burst out furiously. "I must say I think it is reprehensible to mask this endeavor as a charitable effort beneficial to couples who have been deprived of children of their own by bringing these misfits, these cripples, these disabled urchins from the city and try to palm them off on decent folks by playing on their sympathy! We understood these orphans were healthy, strong, ready to work in our homes and fields, to be a blessing not a burden!" She drew herself up indignantly. "Did you really expect to get away with it?"

"I — I don't know what you mean —" stammered Anna. "These children *are* well, perfectly able to do any kind of house or farm work within reason."

The woman stepped aside so that Anna could see around her bulk and pointed across the room. "Then what do you call *those* three!" she demanded with a sniff.

Anna looked in the direction of the pudgy finger, and gasped.

Moving slowly with an exaggerated limp

was Kit, carrying a plateful of food from the table to Toddy, who sat slumped in one of the chairs along the wall, the most horrible expression on her face and her beautiful eyes crossed. Following Kit, Laurel was playing the part of a little hunchback to the hilt.

The woman gave Anna another withering glance, and swept out of the door.

For a moment Anna looked after her helplessly, then with her mouth determinedly set, she started toward the three girls.

"Just what do you think you three are up to?" she asked, trapped between laughter and tears.

Before they could do anything but look back at her with startled, sheepish faces, Anna was beckoned by Matthew to meet a couple ready to take one of the other children.

"We'll see about *this, later!*" Anna promised the trio.

Once back on the train she confronted them. "But *why* would you do such a naughty thing?" she asked severely.

The three little girls were abject, but no one answered.

"Isn't anyone going to tell me the truth?" Anna continued, studying the three downcast faces. "You all know it's sinful to tell lies, don't you? Well, you were all *acting* a lie, pretending something that was not true. That's just as bad. Why, you should get down on your knees and thank God that you're *not* crippled or deformed in any way. Why on earth would three perfectly healthy little girls want to *look* any other way?" Anna asked in frustration.

"Because we didn't want to get adopted!" Toddy burst out.

"*Not* want to be *adopted?*" exclaimed Anna. "But that's the very purpose of this whole trip! It's the reason you were selected to come on this train. You were picked out of dozens of other children at Greystone who would have given anything to come, and now you say you don't want to be adopted!"

"We don't want to be adopted *separately*, Mrs. Scott," explained Kit finally.

"We've made a pact, you see, to be *forever friends*," Laurel added. "We want to be *sure* we get adopted in the same town."

"So we wanted to wait until the *last* town," finished Toddy with satisfaction, as though now everything was understood and accepted.

"So *that's* it!" Anna sighed. At least the mystery was solved. "Who's idea was this —

little charade?" She tried to look stern.

Toddy had the grace to hang her head, but not before Anna spotted that mischievous twinkle in her eyes.

"That was very, *very naughty*," Anna said solemnly, letting her words sink in. Then she turned to the other two. "But going along with it was just as naughty," she scolded. "Remember what happened in the Garden of Eden? Adam sinned as much as Eve when she yielded to the serpent's temptation to eat the forbidden fruit. Adam could have refused to eat the apple, couldn't he? So, you see, you are *all* to blame."

"There *is* only one more town, isn't there, Mrs. Scott?" Toddy asked innocently. "So we won't do that again. But we *do* want to stay together, go to the same school, play together, always be friends. And we figured that wouldn't happen unless we did something about it. We decided it was the best way to keep any one of us from being adopted at some other stop. Don't you see? We thought it was the only way to be *sure*."

"You could have come to me, told me what you wanted to do. You could have trusted me enough to arrange it instead of —"

All three looked remorseful.

"But could you have *promised* us, Mrs.

Scott?" Toddy asked.

When Anna did not answer right away, Toddy shook her head and turned up her palms in a helpless gesture. "You see, we had to be *sure* we stayed together. That's why we did it!"

7

"Meadowridge! Meadowridge! Next stop, Meadowridge!"

That call sent an involuntary shiver down Anna Scott's spine. This was the end of the line, the last stop on the long journey that had carried the trainload of orphans across the country. This stop was the most important one of all. Anna whispered a quick, silent prayer, a repeat of the same urgent one she had sent heavenward for the last two hundred miles.

As her prayer took wing, her eyes instinctively sought out the three little girls most on her mind. They looked like three little angels this morning, she thought, but not without a sinking feeling in the pit of her stomach. With those three — you just never knew!

On the surface everything seemed in order; their faces were shiny clean, fingernails immaculate, hair neatly braided, clothes brushed and tidy. Toddy, Laurel and Kit were sitting demurely, hands folded in their laps waiting for the train to come to a stop. Anna drew in her breath, subconsciously knowing she would be holding it until all three girls were safely "placed out."

Nervously she looked out the window as the train began to slow down. It was beautiful countryside they were traveling through — rolling hills, lush farmland, trees with the pale green haze of budding leaves. Everywhere she looked gave evidence of the coming of spring.

Anna felt her heart lift. Spring had always been her favorite time of year, with its promise of loveliness after the long winter. They had left Boston in a cold rain. Now they were coming to the end of their journey with the hopeful signs of budding life. It must be a good omen.

Immediately the Scripture verse from Philippians 1:6 flashed into Anna's mind: "He who has begun a good work in you will complete it." Surely God would honor His Word and all these orphans would find homes.

The train jolted to a stop and Anna, standing in the middle of the aisle, quickly steadied herself by gripping the back of one of the seats.

The children now knew the routine and got to their feet, ready to move out of the train and line up for survey. Compassion for the ordeal they were facing made Anna wince inwardly.

Hurrying to where Toddy, Laurel and Kit stood, she bent down and looked earnestly into each face. "No games this time!" she whispered.

The three nodded solemnly.

"If I may say so, Mrs. Hale, you'll live to regret it," declared Clara Hubbard with the familiarity of a longtime servant as she watched her mistress put on her hat.

"You may certainly say so, Clara, but I don't agree. I think it is the best possible thing I can do for my granddaughter. Why, you've heard her a dozen times yourself, I'm sure. Over and over. Helene has always said her dearest wish was for a little sister."

"But, ma'am, what kind of a child will you get from an Orphan Train? They drag the city streets for 'em, so I've heard. The very scum from who knows where? And you want to bring one *here*, into your home, *this* house, to live with Miss Helene, the most delicate of creatures!"

"I have outlined very explicitly the kind of child we are looking for, Clara, and I have been assured that the available children are all healthy, bright, personable," Mrs. Hale replied calmly. Then she added, "Besides Helene herself will make the final selection."

Clara folded her arms on the starched bosom of her crisp white apron and sniffed disdainfully.

"And I might add, Clara, once the child enters this house, she is to be treated as one of the family," continued Mrs. Hale, turning around from the mirror where she had been inserting hatpins into her crepe-trimmed bonnet, securing it to her upswept hairdo. Facing her housekeeper she said sternly, "You *do* understand, Clara? Do I make myself clear?"

"Yes, madam, very clear."

"And I expect you to relay my wishes to the rest of the staff." Mrs. Hale picked up her long kid gloves and started to put them on, carefully smoothing each finger as she did so. "Now, will you please go and see if Miss Tuttle has Helene ready to go with me to the train station."

The housekeeper started out, but at the door she paused and turned back for a final word, "You know, don't you, madam, that Miss Tuttle is upset about this. She don't approve of it one bit." With that Clara gave a little self-satisfied nod of her tightly braided gray head and went out.

Mrs. Hale finished buttoning her gloves thoughtfully. Outwardly composed, she had some inner doubts of her own she had not

71

shared with her housekeeper. Was she doing the right thing bringing in a stranger to live as a companion to her frail granddaughter?

But Helene had been ecstatic when Olivia first broached the idea. Now there was no turning back. That is, unless the child proved impossible, as Clara had predicted she might! Her practical, down-to-earth housekeeper was more often right than not. But in this case, Olivia hoped to heaven she was wrong.

Muted voices in the hall alerted her to the fact that her granddaughter and her nurse were approaching. Olivia hurried to the door to meet them.

"You mustn't hurry so, Helene," Miss Tuttle was saying to the slender, dark-haired girl as they came down the curved staircase.

Attired in a blue velvet coat and matching bonnet, Helene was pale with excitement, but her big dark eyes were shining.

"Oh, Grandmother, it's really time, isn't it? I can hardly wait to see my little sister! I wish they'd sent a picture of her so I could pick her out right away. But, of course, they couldn't. They didn't know which one, but *I'll* know her right away, I *know* I will."

"Now, now, Helene!" remonstrated Miss Tuttle, patting the girl's shoulder while throwing a reproving glance at Mrs. Hale. Shaking her head so that the stiff wings of her nurse's cap fluttered, she said, "All this excitement isn't good for Helene. Do you really think she should go down to the train station with all that crowd, all that confusion?"

Olivia looked at Helene with concern.

But immediately Helene protested. "Oh, Grandmother, please! I want to go. I *have* to go!"

"I think it would be far worse for her to stay at home when she has been looking forward so much to this day." Olivia spoke directly to Miss Tuttle. Ignoring the nurse's sour expression, she said soothingly to Helene, "Of course, you're going, dear."

"Oh, thank you, Grandmother. See, Miss Tuttle, it's all right. I feel perfectly fine. And I want to be there when my little sister gets off the train!"

Clara was standing in the background, her brow furrowed in a frown. Although she and the nurse, whom she considered too high and mighty for her position, rarely agreed on anything, this time they had collaborated in their disapproval of this venture.

"Well then, Clara, tell Jepson to bring the carriage around. We want to get to the station in plenty of time before the train arrives." Olivia gave the order firmly so there would be no doubt of her intentions.

"I've got her present, Grandmother. I hope she likes it!" Helene beamed, holding up a brightly wrapped and bowed package.

"I'm sure she will." Olivia smiled fondly at the child. Because of her illness Helene was small for her age and fragile-boned. Her eyes seemed too big for the thin face that seemed almost translucent in its pallor. But her smile was radiant. A smile so like Dick's, the son she had lost so tragically, that it melted Olivia's heart to see it. If only his daughter had inherited his strength and vitality as well, she thought sadly.

So what if the excitement meant Helene would have to stay in bed for a few days after? It was well worth it to see her so happy today.

The Meadowridge Community Church ladies had outdone themselves with a showcase of the best dishes prepared by the best cooks in the congregation. Some of the recipes on hand had been prize winners at the County Fair. Platters of fried chicken, sliced ham, succulent meat loaf, bowls of coleslaw, potato salad, homemade bread and rolls still warm from the oven, cherry, apple and berry pies, walnut bundt cake, lemon pound cake and chocolate layer cake were set on long tables covered with crisp blue-checkered cloths in the church Social Hall.

This delicious sight made the children's eyes widen and their mouths water. For days at a time, their fare aboard the train was limited to what could be safely stored without fear of spoilage. The daily menu consisted mainly of crackers, jam, oatmeal cooked on the small pot-bellied stove at one end of the car, and dried apples. Sometimes Anna doled out small quantities of hard candies from her hoarded supply. But in general, the menu seemed dismally monotonous. Of course, there were times when the train made longer stops and Matthew was able to go into the town to purchase fresh milk or fruit. However, these were at long intervals.

So it was no wonder that for a few long minutes, the children stood staring, wide-eyed, at the feast spread out before them. It wasn't until one enterprising church lady stepped forward and pushed them gently into line that the boys and girls moved forward to accept plates of food dished out by other ladies standing behind the tables.

While the orphans were treated to a feast,

the prospective families were seated around the rooms, watching and murmuring to each other as the children passed before them.

When Toddy was told she would be one of the children designated to go to the Orphan Train out West, she had been filled with excitement. She had packed and repacked the small cardboard suitcase each child was given with the new things issued for the trip and for which each orphan had been made to write a laboriously printed "thank you" note to the Rescuers and Providers Society.

Toddy had been at Greystone longer than either of her two best friends, Kit and Laurel, and although she had seemingly adjusted to the institution, the idea of traveling hundreds of miles by train to a new town and being adopted by a real family sounded like the greatest of adventures to her.

From the time Miss Clinock assembled the selected ones in her office to tell them what was going to happen, Toddy could talk of little else. Subconsciously, she had long ago given up hope that Mazel would ever show up and she would return to the backstage life to which she was accustomed. But neither had she ever completely accepted the fact that she was just like all the rest of the children at Greystone, an abandoned orphan. Toddy's vivid imagination kept creating fairy tales of magical "happy endings" for her future.

But, not even in her wildest dreams, had Toddy expected it to happen so easily and simply as it did.

She was sitting on one of the straight-backed chairs placed around the walls of the Meadowridge Community Church Social Hall, finishing her meal. Because her feet did not quite reach the floor, she hung her heels over the rung to steady herself as she tried to eat daintily. Balancing her plate on her knees was not an easy task — especially when she could feel observant eyes upon her as she took each bite, though Toddy had become fairly used to being watched. "They" had done it often enough, off and on the train at the various stations. Not all the times had been as nice as this one.

Glancing up from her plate, Toddy saw a girl on the other side of the room, looking at her. She was pretty, tall, slim, dressed in a blue dress, with a tucked bodice and pleated skirt. Her dark hair was drawn back from her pale face with a large bow. Her eyes seemed almost too big, but they were sparkling and she was smiling — smiling right at Toddy!

Anna had had every intention of keeping a close watch on Toddy, Laurel and Kit, trying to see that they were never farther than an arm's length away from her supervision lest they forget her stern warnings and revert to their "play-acting" to keep from being separated.

She had even half harbored the fanciful notion that some family would be willing to adopt all three girls. Of course, this was a practical impossibility, Anna told herself, and her chief concern was that each girl *was* "placed out" in a good home. Still, she *did* want to be able to talk to the adoptive parents and tell them how important their friendship was to the little trio.

Anna glanced over to the table at the other end of the hall where Matthew and Reverend Brewster sat conferring. In front of them were all the children's papers containing their vital statistics — birth dates; natural parents' names, if known; place of birth; release forms of availability for adoption signed by one or both parents, or from the orphanage from which they'd come. After making their choices, the adoptive parents would come here to sign the adoption commitment.

Maybe she should remind Matthew of their discussion about the three before any of their papers were signed.

But before she could do so, her attention was diverted by a woman who introduced herself as Mrs. Kingsley, the Chairman of the Ladies' Guild, who immediately launched into a monologue.

"I wasn't sure whether you knew that although Meadowridge is the county seat, we have many families in outlying districts who regularly come here for church, shopping and so on. You'll be glad to know that we sent out announcements of the coming of the Orphan Train to all these areas so I feel sure people will be arriving all day with plans to take some of these poor little ones."

At this information Anna felt a stab of alarm. She had promised the girls they would live close to each other, attend the same school. If they were taken by a family outside Meadowridge, it might be too far, especially in bad weather, for them to come in to school during the winter. She *must* make sure that didn't happen. She had to speak to Matthew. Hurriedly excusing herself, Anna started over to him.

But she had taken only a few steps when she was halted by an imperious voice.

"One minute, if you please, Mrs. Scott."

Anna turned as a handsome woman, elegantly dressed in fashionable black attire, placed a gloved hand on her arm.

"I am Olivia Hale," she said. "You may remember that you and your husband came to tea at my home on your last visit to Meadowridge. I invited you to discuss my adopting a child, a girl, to be a companion to my granddaughter, Helene. At that time I outlined the requirements necessary in such a child because of the special circumstances of my granddaughter's health. I asked that with these in mind, you select a child and bring her with you on this trip for me to meet."

At her words Anna recalled the day vividly. Matthew had received a note from Mrs. Hale — ostensibly an invitation, but more like a summons — to come to the enormous hilltop home, tiered and towered, overlooking the town of Meadowridge. They had been shown into a magnificently furnished parlor where they were met by the lady, as regal as Queen Victoria herself.

They had been served tea poured from a silver pot into delicate china cups while Mrs. Hale described the type of child she wanted for a companion to her granddaughter.

Afterwards Anna and Matthew had discussed the interview.

"She doesn't want a real child!" Anna declared indignantly. "She wants a paragon of virtue, intelligence, and disposition."

"Yes, she does seem to have forgotten, if indeed she ever knew, what most children are like. No matter how obedient, demure or agreeable, they are still flesh and blood little human beings with all the natural flaws and faults we are all disposed to," Matthew replied thoughtfully. "But we can only do our best to find a child who will fit into that situation."

"It sounds impossible!"

Matthew smiled at her. "Remember, 'with God all things are possible.' We'll just pray that we will find exactly the right child for the Hales."

"I wonder what the granddaughter herself is like," mused Anna. "Given those luxurious surroundings, that doting grandmother, she's probably a pampered, spoiled brat."

Anna felt herself flush, recalling her less than charitable comment. In the busy months since that visit, Anna had almost forgotten Mrs. Hale and her specific requirements. Matthew, of course, had conscientiously written them down and put them in his files. Now as it all came back to her Anna immediately thought of one of her special three, Kit Ternan. Kit, with her sweet quiet ways, her sensitivity and spontaneous warmth would make an ideal companion for a semi-invalid. But before Anna could voice her suggestion, a dark-haired girl with shining eyes was tugging at Mrs. Hale's arm.

"Oh, Grandmother, I've found her!" she exclaimed. "My 'little sister.' She's darling. Look, Grandmother, over there! See?"

Both women turned to follow the direction of Helene's pointed finger.

To Anna's amazement, it was Toddy.

While Helene happily took Toddy by the hand and began regaling her with all the things she had planned to do once her "little sister" came to live with her, Olivia went with Mrs. Scott to fill out the adoption agreement papers.

Her concern over her granddaughter's choice must have been evident because Anna began an enthusiastic recommendation of Toddy designed to counteract any fears Mrs. Hale might have.

"Toddy is a delightful child, Mrs. Hale, cheerful and bright. I think she will be a wonderful companion for your granddaughter."

"Not too lively, do you think?" posed Mrs. Hale cautiously.

"Well, she's certainly not dull!" Anna fielded the question adroitly.

After her first surprise at the selection, the more she thought about it, Anna realized that Toddy *was* the right one. For a lonely child such as Helene, confined as she was and sentenced to a life of limited activity, Toddy would be the proverbial breath of fresh air.

Mrs. Hale pursed her lips, withholding comment. She had never yet denied Helene anything it was in her power to give her, and she wasn't about to start now.

But as she looked over the background information on this child Helene had chosen, Olivia almost faltered. She read:

NAME OF CHILD: Zephronia Victorine Todd
BIRTH DATE: June, 1882
Female, White
Hair, Blond
Eyes, Blue   Health: Excellent
MOTHER: Mazel Cooper
OCCUPATION: Dancer
LAST KNOWN ADDRESS: Rialto Theater   No communication since 1886. Child transferred from "Temporary" Status to "Available for Placement" — January 1888.

FATHER: John Todd, Comedic Actor, Song & Dance — Haynes Vaudeville Troupe PRESENT WHEREABOUTS UNKNOWN

Good Heavens! Olivia rolled her eyes, then gamely took the pen and signed the adoption form. Whatever she had gotten herself into, she was determined to see it through. As the Good Book exhorted, having set her hand to the plow, she would not look back. One glance at Helene's smiling face and shining eyes was enough to convince Olivia that however it turned out, this was the only decision she could have made.

"Oh, I'm so glad you've come, Toddy! You can't imagine how I've longed for a little sister," Helene said, once they were settled in the carriage opposite Mrs. Hale. "Oh, Grandmother, isn't Toddy cunning?" Turning to Toddy, she said, "Oh, we are going to have the most wonderful times together. Just wait and see!" And she gave a little bounce of excitement.

Reacting at once to Helene's enthusiasm, Toddy clapped her hands together and gave a corresponding bounce on her side. Helene laughed and then Toddy did and soon they were both laughing merrily as if at some hilarious joke.

Mrs. Hale could not keep her own mouth from lifting in amusement at the two children's delight with each other. Well, maybe it was going to be fine after all, in spite of all Clara's dire predictions and warnings of the dark consequences of bringing a strange child into their lives. Olivia was not given to premonitions, but she had a strong feeling with the arrival of *Zephronia Victorine* that everyone in the Hale household was in for big changes.

8

The first thing Toddy saw when she entered the Hale house was a tall woman wearing a starched white apron, a stiff peaked cap, and a severe expression. She was standing by the staircase in the front hall, arms folded, her foot tapping impatiently. Before Mrs. Hale could say anything, the nurse was at Helene's side, helping her off with her coat, shaking her head.

"Helene looks very flushed, Mrs. Hale. It is my opinion she should go straight to bed and have supper on a tray. I refuse to take the responsibility if she has any more excitement this evening."

"But, I'm not a bit tired, Miss Tuttle!" Helene protested. "And I don't want to leave Toddy on her first night here. Oh, you haven't met Toddy yet, Miss Tuttle. Look, isn't she a darling? Look at her rosy cheeks, her adorable little nose. Isn't she the sweetest thing you've ever seen?"

The subject of this rhapsodic recital smiled hopefully at the nurse hovering over Helene. When the smile was not returned, in fact, was met with a cold stare, Toddy was alerted. This was someone who was not pleased by her arrival. Somewhere Toddy had learned the wisdom of knowing the enemy and in that one chilling moment she recognized hers.

Mrs. Hale looked at her granddaughter anxiously. Helene *did* have unusually high color in her cheeks. There was no use taking chances. After all, she did pay Miss Tuttle a handsome salary to take care of Helene's health. In this case, she would have to rely on her judgment.

"Oh, Grandmother!" wailed Helene. "I feel fine, really I do! Let me stay up for dinner at least! Then I'll go straight to bed. I promise." Helene turned pleading eyes on Olivia, who in turn, exchanged a glance with the frowning Miss Tuttle. She hesitated.

Then unable to resist her granddaughter's plea, Olivia gave in.

"Well, just until after we've had dinner. But then, you must go to bed. It won't do for you to be ill when Toddy has just come. There'll be plenty of time for the two of you to be together, Helene. Toddy is going to be living here from now on. You don't want to be ill tomorrow and not be able to enjoy her company, now do you?" she asked in a reasonable tone of voice.

"Oh, thank you, Grandmother. Come along, Toddy. I want to show you the play-room. When we knew you were coming, we got some toys and games and other things especially —" Helene took Toddy's hand and started upstairs.

"Slowly, Helene!" cautioned Miss Tuttle, hurrying after them. "Don't rush up those steps!" She paused at the foot to cast another reproving look at Mrs. Hale before following the girls.

Ignoring it and her own misgivings, Olivia turned away. Only time would tell if this had been a terrible mistake. Right now all she could see was the happiness in Helene's eyes. She was not going to borrow trouble.

An hour later the three of them were seated in the candlelit dining room, at the long table covered with a creamy linen cloth and set with gleaming silver and crystal. Helene, who had not stopped chatting, took her place with the ease of familiarity, while Toddy's eyes grew large with the newness of things about her.

At Greystone they had lined up and passed along the serving counters with their plates while the meal, whatever it consisted of, was dished out to them. There were no choices, no seconds.

Here, a man in a dark jacket moved silently from the massive buffet over to the table, bringing a number of covered silver serving dishes, one at a time, first to Mrs. Hale, then to Helene. Toddy watched how they each helped themselves from the dishes he held to their left, while they would help themselves with their right hands. When he approached her with a platter of chops, she still felt unsure.

"Would you like me to serve you, miss?" he asked quietly.

She nodded shyly. "Yes, please." Toddy observed as he deftly picked up a chop with silver tongs and placed one on her plate. Next time she would know how.

After that came a silver bowl with a mound of snowy potatoes, then two different kinds of vegetables. Each time, Thomas, as she heard Mrs. Hale call him, would offer her the serving dish for a few seconds, allowing her time to decide if she could manage. He never was obvious about it and, if she seemed uncertain, he then served her a portion.

Toddy was grateful for his discreet help and, when he brought around a covered dish of hot rolls, she gave him one of her best smiles. She couldn't be sure but she thought she saw one eyelid drop briefly in a wink, although his expression remained impassive. Perhaps this kind man would be someone she could count on in this strange new world she had entered.

After she ate the last bite of a creamy caramel custard and the pretty crystal dish was removed, Mrs. Hale told Thomas she would take her coffee in the parlor. At the same time, Miss Tuttle appeared at the door.

"Time for you to go up now, Helene," Mrs. Hale said in a tone that brooked no argument.

Reluctantly Helene slipped from her chair, went over to Toddy and hugged her impulsively.

"Good night, Toddy. I'll see you in the morning." At the door she paused and looked back longingly. "I'm so glad you're here!"

After Helene left Mrs. Hale rose. "Come along, Toddy, we need to get acquainted."

A cheerful fire was burning in the fireplace, the curtains drawn and the lamps with ruby glass globes on the marble-topped tables had been lighted. Mrs. Hale took a seat in one of the chairs by the fireplace and indicated Toddy should take the matching one on the other side.

"Toddy, there are a few things you must remember now that you will be living here.

The first is that although Helene may seem fine to you, she has a very weak heart and she must not get overexcited. So you will have to be careful what games you suggest playing. She wants to please so very much that she sometimes extends her strength and then gets very ill. When that happens, the doctor has to be summoned and — well, I think you understand what I'm saying."

Toddy, her hands folded in her lap, nodded gravely.

"Mrs. Scott told me you were a very smart little girl, that you learned quickly. So, I'm relying on you to follow both my orders and whatever Miss Tuttle, Helene's nurse, suggests. Remember, it is for Helene's good."

"Yes, ma'am, I'll remember," Toddy replied, her round little face very serious.

"Good." Mrs. Hale seemed satisfied.

The parlor door opened and Thomas brought in a tray bearing Mrs. Hale's coffee and set it down on the table in front of her.

"Will there be anything else, ma'am?"

"Not for me, Thomas. But ask Mrs. Hubbard to come in, please." After Thomas went out, she said to Toddy, "It's been a long, tiring day for all of us, and especially for you, Toddy, so I think you should go to bed. Our housekeeper will show you to your room, which is right next to Helene's. She's probably asleep by now, so you won't disturb her, will you?"

A knock sounded on the door, and Mrs. Hale called, "Come in, Clara." A stout, gray-haired woman bustled in. She cast a curious, unsmiling look in Toddy's direction, then stood a few feet from Mrs. Hale and waited.

"Mrs. Hubbard, this is Toddy who will be staying with us, as you know. Would you kindly take her upstairs, show her where she's to sleep, and get her settled?"

"Yes, ma'am." The woman nodded, turned and walked briskly to the door. There she speared Toddy with a rapier glance. "Come along."

"Good night, Toddy, sleep well," Mrs. Hale called out as Toddy got down from the chair and followed the housekeeper out of the room.

Clara never looked back to see if anyone was behind her. She just marched up the wide staircase with Toddy hurrying to keep up. At the landing the housekeeper made a turn and went down a long corridor. At the end, she paused at a door and held it open for Toddy, who was trotting as fast as she could down the hallway.

Toddy stepped in and stood, looking around in awe. The bedroom seemed immense, partly because there was only *one* bed instead of dozens of cots. There was a dresser with a tall mirror and two plumply cushioned chairs covered in flowered material, the same as the curtains that were pulled over a curved bank of windows on one side of the room.

Toddy spotted her battered suitcase, very much the worse for wear from the cross-country train trip. It looked somehow forlorn, even if familiar, in the midst of all this luxury.

The housekeeper was turning down the crocheted coverlet on the high bed and fluffing up the ruffled pillows.

"Well, I suppose you have something to sleep in, don't you?" she asked abruptly.

Toddy started over to the suitcase. She really hated to get out the rumpled flannel nightie which she had worn so long and with no chance to launder it — particularly under the sharp eyes of the housekeeper. Everything here looked so new.

"What kind of a name is *Toddy* anyway?" Mrs. Hubbard asked sharply. "Don't you have a decent, Christian name?"

"I've just always been called Toddy." She shrugged. "But my *real* written-out name is Zephronia Victorine."

At this Mrs. Hubbard threw up her hands

in a hopeless gesture.

"For mercy sakes! What can people be thinkin' of to dream up such as *that!*" Then, taking one look at the wrinkled nightgown Toddy had lifted out of the suitcase, she gave a huge sigh. "No, that will never do! You can't wear that rag of a thing into a bed that's just been made up fresh. You'll have to wear one of Helene's, even if it does swallow you." She put her hands on her hips and scrutinized Toddy. "I think you'll be needing a bath, too."

Toddy's cheeks flamed with embarrassment under Mrs. Hubbard's critical gaze.

Seeing the little girl turn red, the housekeeper hurried to take the edge off her words. After all, it wasn't the child's fault that her clothes had been packed all that long time. Land sakes, they'd traveled clear across the country, she reminded herself.

Clara Hubbard was a realist. Although she had disapproved of the plan to take in one of the children from the Orphan Train, now that it was a fact of life, she might as well make the best of it. Besides, the child seemed a spunky little tyke. There was no call to be so sharp with her.

"Wait 'till you see the bathroom in this house!" she told Toddy, beckoning her to follow as she opened the door and went out into the hall again.

Five minutes later Toddy was seated in a froth of soapy bubbles in the biggest tub she had ever seen. When Clara had shown her the bathroom, Toddy was speechless. It was every bit as big as the bedroom. Besides the gleaming bathtub with its lion's claw legs set on a platform, there was a porcelain wash-bowl on a pedestal and a rack beside it, laden with thick towels of every size, edged with cotton lace and embroidered with the initials *OH*. With pride Mrs. Hubbard assured her the rest of the "necessities" were the very latest in modern plumbing.

Using a huge sponge, Mrs. Hubbard scrubbed Toddy until she was pink and tingling all over, then shampooed her hair and vigorously dried it. Finally, puffing with the exertion, the housekeeper dropped the sweet-smelling, lace-trimmed nightgown over Toddy's head, and helped her climb up into the tall bed where she sank into its feathery depths.

Standing over her, Mrs. Hubbard declared, "Well, then, you're all settled. Next time, you can do for yourself, a big girl like you." She spread the quilt over Toddy, then picked up the lamp and went to the door. "So, good night to you."

She went out, taking the light with her

and closed the door, leaving Toddy staring into the dark.

Toddy heard the housekeeper's firm footsteps fading as she went down the hall and then everything seemed very quiet. Too quiet. Used to sleeping in a dormitory with dozens of sounds — the sound of others breathing, turning over, coughing, muffled whispers, the squeak of bedsprings — to Toddy the deep silence seemed eerie.

For the first time in her life, Toddy was alone. And she didn't like it. She missed the comforting sense of her companions on either side. She longed to reach out her hand and feel Kit's — or Laurel's responding clasp. She wondered where each of them was tonight and if they, too, were lonely and did they miss *her* as much as she missed them?

There came a stinging rush of tears into her eyes. They rolled down her cheeks and saltily into her mouth. Much as she tried to check them, sobs began to fill her throat and she could not hold them back. She stuffed the end of the sheet into her mouth. Still they came.

But Toddy had learned early that tears never brought an end to what caused them. She turned over, burying her head in the soft, lavender-scented pillows. It would be all right, she told herself. Tomorrow she would see Helene again. Helene had promised they would be "sisters." Tomorrow would be the beginning of that "happily ever after" Toddy had always longed for.

9

Whatever Toddy had expected her life at the Hales to be, she soon discovered it was not going to be a fairy tale.

It soon became quite clear that except for Helene, her presence was resented.

Mrs. Hale, a remote figure who remained at some distance, tolerated her for Helene's sake, but the rest of the household made plain their feelings in various ways.

The day after Toddy's arrival, Helene awakened with a fever and Dr. Woodward had to be sent for. There was a great deal of rushing about up and down the halls as Miss Tuttle issued orders.

Miss Tuttle, now fully in charge, made it known in no uncertain terms what she felt had brought on Helene's fever.

Downstairs, Mrs. Hale awaited Dr. Woodward's verdict. Obviously concerned about her granddaughter, she did not even seem to see Toddy.

For the next few days everything in the Hale residence centered on Helene. Meals were served by a distracted maid named Paula in the small morning room adjoining the big dining room where they had eaten the first night. Other than that, nobody paid any particular attention to Toddy. She only caught glimpses of Mrs. Hale who seemed to pace the upstairs hall outside Helene's room most of the time. Either she wasn't eating or else having her meals served in her own suite at the other end of the hall from Helene's room where she kept an anxious vigil.

Always self-reliant, Toddy occupied herself. This was not hard to do because Helene had provided many new books and games in anticipation of her arrival. The trouble was, most of the toys and games required partners or opponents.

Toddy wandered about listlessly, wishing she knew exactly where Kit and Laurel had been "placed out." But there was so much last-minute confusion at the church social hall after Helene had claimed her that Toddy had not had a chance to find out her friends' whereabouts.

It had all happened so fast Toddy's head was spinning. The next thing she knew they had been rolling along the streets of Meadowridge in the Hale carriage up the hill to the castlelike house where Toddy would live with her new family.

The afternoon of the second day of

Helene's confinement, Toddy became rest-less. It was a beautiful sunny day and much too nice to stay inside. Unnoticed, she slipped downstairs and out the side door into the garden.

It was every bit as big as the playground at Greystone, Toddy realized as she looked around. There were narrow gravel paths winding between colorfully blooming flower beds. Toddy recognized some of the flowers from the arrangement in the bowl in the center of the dining room table; others she had seen in vases throughout the house. She had never seen so many different kinds of flowers. She walked around, stopping to touch them gently, to bend down here and there to inhale their sweet scent.

Then she saw a man in overalls busily trimming the hedges against a spiked iron fence that rose at the outside edge of the garden. Eager for a chance to talk to someone, Toddy skipped over and greeted him cheerfully.

"Hello!"

He turned a scowling face to glance down at her and went on snipping with his wide pointed shears.

"I've come to live here," Toddy told him.

No answer.

"I came all the way 'cross the country in a

train," she said next hoping to pique his interest.

Another grunt. The snippers moved without stopping.

"My name's Toddy. What's your name?"

"Ferrin," he growled.

"I'm going to be Helene's little sister," she said brightly, moving along with him as he went to the next hedge.

At this he turned and gave her a hard look. "You're one of them orphans, ain't you? Come on the train?"

"Yes!" she nodded, smiling.

"Well, wouldn't be gettin' no fancy ideas if I wuz you," he said. "Blood's thicker'n water. Make no mistake 'bout that."

Toddy was puzzled. What did he mean? she wondered. As Ferrin moved forward, she fell into step beside him, ready to pursue his enigmatic remark. But he turned toward her, brandishing his shears.

"Now, go along with you! I'm busy. Don't have time for gabbin'. Got my work to do."

Taken aback by this abrupt dismissal, Toddy whirled around and started down the path in the opposite direction. At the far end was an elaborately fashioned gazebo with a pointed roof and latticed sides. Curious, Toddy headed for it.

What a wonderful place this would be to play in, she thought. It would make a great stage for pantomimes and little skits, if only there were someone to play with, she thought.

Just then she saw a boy's face, topped by a tousled head of tawny hair, peering over the fence at her.

"Who are you?" she gasped.

"Chris Blanchard. Who are you?"

"I'm Toddy. What are you doing there?"

"I'm climbing trees in ole Mr. Traherne's orchard. What are you doing over there?"

"I live here,"she replied.

"Since when? Nobody but rich ole Mrs. Hale lives in *that* house," he retorted.

"Not any more. *I* live here and so does Helene."

"Who's Helene?"

"She's my sister. We're sisters and I do *so* live here!"

Chris seemed to be considering that fact. Then he asked, "Wanna play?"

It was just exactly what Toddy wanted to do.

"Sure!"

"Can you climb trees?" he asked doubtfully.

"Of course."

"Well, come on then."

But first Toddy had to figure a way out of the Hales' garden. She was so intent on proving that she not only could climb trees but could also scale the fence into the orchard, that it never entered her mind to ask anyone's permission to go.

It was only an hour later when she climbed back over the fence, minus her hair ribbon, with her dress dirty and sticky with resin, her stockings torn and her shoes scuffed, that she realized she was in trouble.

She and Chris had had a great time climbing one after the other of the low-hanging branches of the gnarled, twisted old trees in Traherne's apple orchard. Chris had turned out to be a jolly fellow once he saw Toddy could match his athletic prowess. He had shared with her some crumbled gingerbread he had stashed in his pocket while they exchanged vital information. They found out they were the same age and would, come September, Chris told her, both be in Miss Cady's class at Meadowridge Grammar School.

It was only at the sound of Clara Hubbard's irritated voice calling her name that Toddy hurriedly said goodbye to Chris and scrambled down from the tree and back over the fence into the garden.

There she found Mrs. Hubbard, hands on

her hips, glaring at her as she slid down.

"Well, if you aren't a sight!" she declared. "We've been looking all over for you. Mrs. Hale's been that worried. She thought you'd run away or something. Not that that would worry me none. Come along. Let's get you cleaned up. Helene's feeling better and has been asking for you."

She grabbed Toddy by the arm and pulled her along toward the house. Toddy knew she was in disgrace. But the afternoon had been worth it. Chris was fun, for a boy. And Helene would like to hear all about her adventure, Toddy was sure.

"More trouble than it's worth!" mumbled Mrs. Hubbard as she swiped the dirt off Toddy's face with a damp washcloth. "And what in the world will we put on you?" she demanded irritably.

Instinctively, Toddy knew Mrs. Hubbard was a friend she needed and she looked up into the flushed, frowning face and smiled, saying sweetly, "I'm sorry."

Mrs. Hubbard felt an unexpected thaw in the icy reserve she maintained. In spite of all the extra work this child was giving, there *was* something cherubic in that uplifted face.

"Oh, well, children will be children, I suppose," she sighed resignedly. And maybe after all it would be good for Helene to have this lively little person around. "Now, you're presentable, so go along with you. Helene's been frettin' to see you."

Toddy hurried along to Helene's room where Miss Tuttle stood sentinel at the door.

"Now, you're not to tire Helene, you understand," she said severely.

"No, ma'am," Toddy answered meekly knowing that she might have won over Mrs. Hubbard, but Miss Tuttle was still a formidable hurdle.

10

On doctor's orders Helene had to stay in bed for the remainder of the week. But Toddy was allowed to spend a good deal of time with her. She learned this privilege was at Helene's insistence and with Mrs. Hale's reluctant consent, despite the advice of Miss Tuttle.

"Now you mustn't tire Helene" was the repeated caution.

How in the world could you tire someone who was sitting up in bed on mounds of ruffled pillows propped against its curlicued headboard, playing Parcheesi? Toddy, sitting cross-legged at the foot of Helene's high, shiny brass and white enameled bed, the board game between them, pondered the question.

Helene's room was the grandest Toddy had ever seen. Carpeted in soft green with designs of large roses in pale pink, its tall windows were curtained with white dotted Swiss tied back with enormous pink taffeta bows. Wallpapered in patterns of trellised roses, the room blossomed like a garden bower. On a pink marble-topped table beside Helene's bed was a tall lamp with a beautiful glass shade with painted roses on it.

Dominating one side of the room were bookcases filled with books, more than the orphanage library! Facing these on a long table was a large globe of the world. This was where Helene had lessons when she was well. A lady came to teach her at home since she wasn't strong enough to attend regular school, she had told Toddy.

A door opened out onto a little balcony with a cushioned lounge chair for Helene to lie on and white wicker chairs and a matching table where she had lunch on warm, sunny days. The trays were brought up by Paula, the maid, who would have been pretty except for her sullen expression and a mouth in a perpetual pout.

Toddy was puzzled about Paula. She tried smiling at her every time she saw her — whether in Helene's room or when they passed on the stairs. But the maid only tossed her head and turned away, never speaking. It bothered Toddy to feel Paula didn't like her for some reason. But, then, the most important thing was that Helene *did*.

And Toddy had loved Helene right from the beginning. Who could help loving someone who thought you were adorable, who laughed at everything funny you said, and wanted to hear all about you?

For some reason Toddy wasn't sure she should tell Helene about her life before Greystone. That life had become rather vague even in her own mind in the last two years, almost like a dream, or something that had happened to someone else. The Carellis, Flo and the other dancers, even her mother, Mazel, had faded into the gray regions of memory. It was only every once in a while, mostly when she was drifting off to sleep at night, that Toddy would remember something about that life — a snatch of a song she had learned by listening to it every night from the wings, or the flash of the vivacious Donna and Doug, a "song and dance" team, who were always so nice to her.

Anyway, what Helene was mainly curious about was Greystone. She wanted to know what it was like in an orphanage, a place she had only read about in stories.

"You know, Toddy, *I'm* an orphan, too," Helene confided one day. "If it weren't for Grandmother, I would probably have been put in an orphanage just like you. My mother and father are both dead. I hardly remember either of them."

Toddy almost said that *she* wasn't *actually* an orphan, that *her* parents weren't dead. But she bit her tongue. For at Greystone she had long ago stopped saying, "My mother is coming to get me soon," especially after Molly B. had taunted her about being moved from the "temporary" to "available for placement" list in Miss Clinock's office. Toddy *knew* Mazel wasn't dead and that her father was "somewhere," though she had not the slightest idea *where.*

But Helene seemed to like the idea that they were *both* orphans. That fact seemed to bring them closer, make them more like *real* sisters. And whatever made Helene happy, Toddy began to understand, was what was important in the Hale household. As long as Helene was happy, Toddy's place was secure.

So Toddy began to regale Helene with stories about Greystone, some true, some she made up, embellished with fine dramatic flair.

"So did you have many friends there?" Helene questioned her.

"Well, I had two special ones," Toddy told her. "Kit and Laurel. They got 'placed out' here in Meadowridge, too. I guess we'll all be in the same class at school."

"Oh, do you know who took them? Where

they are?" asked Helene excitedly.

"No-o-o," Toddy drawled. "I wish I did. I'd like to see them."

"Well, Grandmother can find out!" Helene exclaimed. "Then maybe we can have them over —"

"Really? That would be fun!" Toddy gave a little bounce, upsetting the Parcheesi board, and they both laughed. As they began picking up the markers, Toddy said, "You'll like Laurel and Kit, Helene. At Greystone we —" she halted, then leaning forward and lowering her voice, she asked conspiratorily, "Want me to tell you a secret?"

"Yes, of course. I *love* secrets," Helene assured her, even though she had never had one to keep before.

"You mustn't tell anyone —" Toddy began — "though, I guess it doesn't matter anymore. And Mrs. Scott found out about it anyway." Then Toddy proceeded to describe how the three of them had worked out a plan to avoid adoption until the last stop on the cross-country trip, to insure they would all three stay in the same town.

"Oh, Toddy, if you aren't the limit! The whole thing was *your* idea, wasn't it?" Helene giggled.

Toddy dimpled and nodded. "But we *had*

to do it, Helene. You see at Greystone we promised each other we'd be 'forever friends' and there wasn't any other way."

As it turned out, Toddy was to see Laurel and Kit sooner than she expected. Part of the agreement when The Rescuers and Providers Society "placed out" a child in a home was the stipulation that the children would receive a Christian upbringing and regularly attend Sunday school. To Toddy's delight when Mrs. Hale left her in the Sunday school room at church the following week, the first child she saw was Laurel.

But earlier that morning there had been the first of many incidents with Miss Tuttle that subsequently would not endear her to Helene's nurse.

Since Helene was still running a low-grade fever, she would not be accompanying her grandmother and Toddy to church that Sunday. But Helene had a surprise for Toddy — a new dress and hat for her to wear, purchased in secret by Mrs. Hubbard after Toddy's arrival. Helene told Toddy to come in after her bath and finish dressing in her room before leaving for church.

Helene eagerly watched Toddy's eyes widen as she pushed aside the tissue paper

111

in the big box, kept hidden until that moment. Almost reverently she lifted out the white serge "middy" dress, trimmed in dark blue braid, with a pleated skirt and a red scarf for the collar. The white straw "sailor" hat had long blue streamers. There were white stockings and white buttoned shoes to complete the outfit.

Standing there in her cotton camisole fastened with buttons onto ruffled bloomers, Toddy was speechless. "Oh, Helene!" Toddy said in hushed tones as she held up the dress.

"Well, go ahead, try it on!" urged Helene, pleased at Toddy's delight.

Toddy looked at her, eyes sparkling mischievously, then jammed the straw hat on her head and went into a spontaneous little "sailor's jig." Without missing a beat, she started singing:

> "When I was a lad, I served a term,
> As office boy to an Attorney's firm,
> I cleaned the windows and I swept the
> floor,
> And I polished up the handle of the big
> front door.
> I polished up the handle so carefulee,
> that now I am the Ruler of the Queen's
> Navee!"

Helene laughed and clapped her hands.

"Oh, Toddy, that's marvelous! It's from *Pinafore*, isn't it? Grandmother took me to see it when we were in San Francisco last year!"

Encouraged by her enthusiastic audience, Toddy did another verse and another until a razor-sharp voice sliced through the song, "Stop! Stop that at once, you irreverent child!"

Toddy stopped mid-jig and turned to see Miss Tuttle standing in the doorway. Her flushed face was the picture of outrage, her eyes bulged in indignation, even the starched wings of her nurse's cap bristled. "Need I remind you that this is the Sabbath? I'm shocked, positively shocked. And you, Helene. I'm appalled at you condoning such a vulgar performance. And on *Sunday* too!"

But Helene did not look in the least shocked, Miss Tuttle noticed as she bustled over to her bedside, carrying a tray with her medication on it.

"But, Miss Tuttle, it's from a Gilbert and Sullivan operetta, the Admiral's song from *Pinafore*!" Helene came to Toddy's defense. "The composers are very famous. One writes the music; the other, the words to the songs. All their musical plays are very popular in England. Even members of the Royal

Family have attended them. Isn't Toddy clever to know all the words? To be able to sing like that?"

Miss Tuttle suppressed the angry rebuttal that sprang to her lips. She might have known Helene would defend the little street urchin Mrs. Hale had brought into this house. She probably sang for pennies on city streets before she was rescued and taken to an orphanage. And that's where she should have remained, in Miss Tuttle's opinion. From the first she had heard of it, she had thought that it was a foolish risk, a mistaken act of charity bringing these children out West on the train, palming them off on gullible people, placing them in decent homes, with no thought of the effect. She had said as much to Mrs. Hubbard. She was astonished that a sensible woman like Mrs. Hale would agree to it. But, then, she would do *anything* for Helene, even something as foolhardy as this!

But *this* vulgarity was going too far! Miss Tuttle had learned about the child's background from Clara Hubbard, who had seen the adoption release papers Mrs. Hale had signed, and she had been stunned. What could you expect of someone who came from that sort of life! Her parents — *vaudeville performers!*

114

Yes, Miss Tuttle assured herself, when she reported *this incident,* Mrs. Hale would certainly see her mistake in allowing this child to associate with her granddaughter.

Miss Tuttle pressed her lips together primly. She poured out the thick, syrupy medication into a spoon and offered it to Helene who took it submissively. Filling a tumbler with water, she handed that to her as well. Then she turned to Toddy.

"Take your things into your own room, young lady," she said sharply, "and finish getting dressed without delay."

Miss Tuttle busied herself straightening Helene's covers, thinking all the while just what she would say to Mrs. Hale.

Behind her back the girls exchanged smiles and winks, but Toddy left.

Later, in replaying for Mrs. Hale the shocking scene in Helene's room, Miss Tuttle could not have been more disappointed at her employer's reaction. To her chagrin, Mrs. Hale had listened impassively to the recital, then passed the entire matter off as unimportant. She even seemed annoyed that Miss Tuttle had brought it to her attention.

"But — but aren't you even going to reprimand the girl?" Miss Tuttle gasped.

"Reprimand?" Mrs. Hale frowned,

seeming not to understand the question.

"Punish her for breaking the Sabbath in such an outrageous way? Singing music hall songs and dancing?"

"I don't think the incident calls for any sort of punishment, Miss Tuttle. Evidently, Toddy was entertaining Helene, and Helene was enjoying it very much. So if I punished one, I must punish the other, and I have no intention of doing either."

"But, madam, aren't you concerned about the bad influence this child might have on Helene?" protested Miss Tuttle.

"I think Toddy has been a very good influence on Helene, Miss Tuttle," Mrs. Hale said coolly. "I've never seen Helene as happy or heard her laugh so much as she has since Toddy has come." A smile softened her firm mouth as she continued in an effort to placate the irate nurse. "I even think the Lord Himself might approve, Miss Tuttle. Making a sick child happy is all I see Toddy doing. She is helping Helene in ways all the doctors I've consulted, all the medicines, the care and attention she has had, have not. If I remember my Proverbs correctly, isn't there something about a 'merry heart doing good like medicine'? I believe Toddy is 'good medicine' for Helene."

Miss Tuttle retreated, but she was undaunted in her own conviction that bringing this disruptive child into her well-ordered domain was a dreadful mistake. Mrs. Hale would rue the day, Miss Tuttle was sure.

As she walked haughtily out of the parlor where she had confronted her employer with her indignant report, Miss Tuttle's thoughts were in turmoil. She had never been so humiliated. In other homes where she had done private duty nursing, her word was law. But Mrs. Hale had dismissed her as she might have an ordinary servant — as if she might have been Paula!

If the position did not pay so well, she thought, she would give notice. And, *of course,* if she weren't *absolutely* devoted to Helene. No, it was her duty to stay here and try, somehow, to combat the influence of that child.

Oblivious that she had incurred the wrath of a determined adversary, Toddy blithely entered Sunday school and found herself an immediate success. Lively, bright, and enthusiastic, Toddy was always the first to volunteer to hand out the weekly Sunday school tracts, collect papers, pick up crayons. The teacher, Glenda Harrington, who had been a little apprehensive of the addition of three of the Orphan Train children into her class, was amazed.

At the mid-point, when the class treat of milk and graham squares was served, the three girls shared information about their new homes. Kit was living on a farm just outside town, the only girl in a family of five boys, and Laurel told them that the doctor who had examined them upon their arrival had taken her home with him to be "his little girl." Toddy, of course, had the most to tell about Helene and her new life at the Hales'.

When Miss Harrington lined up the children to re-enter the church for the final hymn and benediction, Toddy noticed Chris Blanchard, her tree-climbing companion in the Traherns' orchard the week before, in the middle of the boys' line. She almost didn't recognize him in his white shirt with his unruly hair slicked down. When she smiled at him, he looked blank, then stuck out his tongue, his face turning scarlet. Toddy shrugged. Boys!

After her reunion with her friends, Toddy looked forward to Sundays. Sometimes Helene felt well enough to go to church, but she sat with her grandmother for the service because there was no class for her age group. Most often, only Toddy accompanied Mrs. Hale in the grand carriage each Sunday.

By the Fourth of July Toddy had been at

the Hale home nearly six weeks. She had no idea what a big celebration this holiday was until the week before.

They were having lunch in the small, sunny breakfast room, with all the windows open to the garden letting in the soft June air, when Helene said to Mrs. Hale, "But Toddy shouldn't miss all the fun just because I can't go, Grandmother. Couldn't Paula take her to the park so she can see the parade and play some of the games? Then Toddy could stay with the Woodwards who adopted her friend Laurel. I'm *sure* they're going and I'm *sure* they wouldn't mind having Toddy. In fact, they'd probably like for Laurel to have someone to be with. Please, Grandmother!"

Toddy looked from one to the other expectantly.

"Well, the servants *do* have the day off —" said Mrs. Hale slowly. "We'll ask Paula if she would take Toddy —" She lifted the small silver bell by her plate and tinkled it gently. Paula appeared as if by magic. She dropped a little curtsy.

"Yes, madam?"

"Paula, we were wondering if you would take Toddy along with you over to the park on the Fourth of July? After the parade you can leave her with Dr. and Mrs. Woodward who will be picnicking there."

Toddy, watching Paula hopefully, thought she detected a look of dismay as the maid darted a quick glance at her. But her only outward reaction was a bob. "Of course, madam."

"Thank you, Paula. It's settled then. I'll send a note to Mrs. Woodward with you," Mrs. Hale said, picking up her spoon and returning to her fruit compote.

Helene's back was to the doorway where Paula stood so no one else saw her eyes narrow into daggers as she glared at Toddy. It was such a cutting look that Toddy shrank back into her seat. She wished the subject had not even been brought up. She'd almost rather not go than have Paula so angry about taking her.

In the rush of excitement about the Fourth, Toddy eventually forgot that moment of fear. The children in Sunday school were full of talk of the races, games, and the concession booths at the park on the big day. And there would be firecrackers, too, and sparklers and the big display put on by the town once it got dark, with Catherine wheels and Roman candles.

Finally the day arrived and when Toddy went into Helene's room early in the morning, a slight feeling of apprehension returned. Climbing up on Helene's bed, she asked anxiously, "Are you sure you don't mind my going?" Her blue eyes were troubled.

"No, of course, not, Toddy! I *want* you to go! I've been a few times and it's lots of fun. Besides, Grandmother says you can invite Laurel and Kit to come home with you and we can all watch the big fireworks from my balcony. She's already checked with Mrs. Woodward, and Laurel can come. You're to ask Kit when you see her at the park. The family who adopted her will be there. *Nobody* in Meadowridge would miss the Fourth of July celebration."

"You're *really* sure? I don't like leaving you here all day by yourself."

"Yes! *Yes!* I'm *sure.*" Helene laughed. "Go on, get ready. Paula will want to leave early since it's her day off."

Since Toddy had never seen Paula wearing anything but her prim, blue-striped uniform and apron, she thought she looked especially pretty in a ruffled shirtwaist — a red checked skirt with a wide belt cinching her small waist — and a shiny straw hat wreathed with red poppies.

Toddy had to trot to keep up with Paula as she hurried down the stairs, out through the kitchen, along the garden path, and through the back gate. Once out of sight of the house, Paula grabbed Toddy's arm and gave her a good shake.

"Now, listen, you little pest! I'm only taking you as far as the park! I'm meeting my own friends and I'm not spoiling *my* day by havin' you tag along. You're plenty big enough to take care of yourself. And you're not to say a word about it to Miss Helene or Mrs. Hale, you understand?" she hissed. "You think you're better'n me, livin' upstairs like you were somethin' when you're nuthin'. Nuthin' at all. Just becuz Miss Helene took a fancy to you don't mean you're special, 'cause you ain't!" Her grip tightened painfully. "If anything happens to *her* you'd be out on your ear, quicker'n you can say Jack Robinson! You'd have to go beggin' like you probably did afore you come! Or worse still, be somebody's skivvy if you're lucky, peelin' spuds and havin' nuthin' to eat but the skins, and sleepin' in the cellar with rats!"

Paula's face was all red with the exertion of her vicious attack.

"So you better listen good to what I'm sayin' or you'll be sorry, you hear me?"

Toddy nodded, feeling the cruel pinch of Paula's fingers on her upper arm.

"So come on." Paula let her go, straightened her hat, which had come askew while she had been delivering her diatribe, then started down the shady sidewalk toward the park, with Toddy following behind.

The day had darkened miserably. Paula's words hung like a weighted chain around Toddy's shoulders. She knew Paula meant every word and that the maid probably was right. Toddy's future was as fragile as Helene's health.

Afterward, a shadow had fallen on the bright sunshine in which Toddy seemed to move. Although within months Paula had left the Hales' employ to marry and move away from Meadowridge, those heedless words spoken in anger etched themselves on Toddy's subconscious mind and remained there long after her childhood.

11

January 1891
Mrs. Anna Scott
c/o The Rescuers and Providers Society

Dear Mrs. Scott,
In compliance with the requirement in the provisional adoption agreement I signed for the housing, care, and welfare of the female orphan, Zephronia Victorine Todd, I herewith submit a progress report.

The above-mentioned child, called "Toddy" has in all respects adjusted well in our household. She is of cheerful disposition, obedient and eager to please. My granddaughter Helene, for whom Toddy has functioned as companion, is very fond of her. They spend many happy hours together, playing, talking and reading. Helene tells me Toddy is very bright and loves to look at travel picture books, wanting to learn about foreign countries and other peoples. She seems to absorb and retain a great deal of what she reads and can converse quite well about the things she is learning.

Although my granddaughter's delicate health requires her to be tutored at home, Toddy entered the local school in September in a combination fourth and fifth class. Her first report card at mid-term showed high grades in Elocution, Composition, Botany, weaker marks in Arithmetic and History. These, her teacher assures me, should improve as her concentration and reading skills progress.

Olivia's flowing script slowed, then paused. Her pen poised, she rested her chin upon her hand and looked out the window beyond her desk. Should she say anything about the day Toddy had come home from school, her face smudged with dirt and tears, her hair ribbons gone, her dress mud-stained and rumpled?

Mrs. Hubbard had come to Olivia in a state quite unlike her usual placid self. Looking up from her needlepoint, Olivia had asked the housekeeper for an account.

"Well, ma'am, it seems Toddy got into some trouble in school."

"What kind of trouble?" Olivia frowned.

Clara looked uncomfortable. "A fight,

ma'am, on the playground. Her teacher has sent home a note."

"Well, then, let me see it."

Clara reached in her apron pocket and drew out a folded piece of paper, handing it to Mrs. Hale.

Olivia's eyes raced over the few lines.

"It doesn't seem all that serious. Miss Cady doesn't say whose fault it was, just that I should question Toddy about it and make it clear to her that such things as kicking and hitting are unacceptable behavior." Olivia looked up from the note. "But I'm sure Toddy knows that already. Was she hurt?"

"No ma'am, but —" Clara hesitated, "I think she gave the Blanchard boy a bloody nose."

"Bernice Blanchard's son?"

Clara nodded.

"My word!" exclaimed Mrs. Hale. "What was it all about, do you know?"

"The most I could get out of her was some of the children began taunting Toddy's friends, the two other little Orphan Train girls — well, Toddy rushed to their defense, it seems. Just plunged into whoever was doing the teasing — I don't know how the Blanchard boy got mixed up in it —"

"Very well, Clara. I'm sure it will all

straighten itself out."

Mrs. Hale's pen began to move again.

"Toddy is very loyal to people she cares about," Olivia wrote.

She had almost forgotten the unpleasant scene with Bernice Blanchard, who had come storming up to the house demanding to see Olivia and had flown into a tirade.

Olivia smiled to herself somewhat grimly. It had been a "tempest in a teapot" certainly, but the underlying prejudice had to be confronted. She had made her own feelings very clear when she had scoffed at Bernice's making a fuss. But later she had made a trip to the school to talk to Miss Cady. She suggested it might be well to talk to the whole class about the virtue of charity, the importance of acceptance, fairness and kindness to one another.

Since then there seemed to have been no more trouble of that sort. At least, if there was, Toddy never mentioned it and her school life seemed to go along smoothly.

Once more Mrs. Hale began to write.

"Toddy has settled in well, has friends at school, gets along with apparent ease with everyone with whom she has contact. We feel she will continue her present progress.

"Our holidays were very pleasant. My granddaughter was excited about having a young child in the house this year, so Helene took great delight in planning many secret surprises for Toddy. She was particularly anxious to make this Christmas special since Toddy confided she had never had a 'real' Christmas. We had a tall evergreen on our property cut and brought in for the girls to decorate. They spent days making circles of gilt paper chains and strings of cranberries and popcorn to drape on the tree. Then we ordered ornaments from a mail catalog to hang, as well.

"On Christmas Eve we attended the program at the church put on by the Sunday school children, then came home to open the presents that had been placed under the tree."

Olivia stopped writing again, thinking about the scene that night.

The spicy scent of the tall cedar, heightened by the warmth of the house, filled the parlor with its fragrance. Thomas and Mrs. Hubbard had hurried to light all the candles when they heard the carriage wheels on the drive outside so that when Mrs. Hale and the girls came in, the sweeping branches of the tree were ablaze with light.

Her eyes, wide and brilliant, her mouth a round O, Toddy stood on the threshold, unable to move or speak.

"Go on, Toddy, don't you want to open your presents?" Helene urged, eager to see her reactions to all the surprises she had chosen for her "little sister."

There were wonderful books, games, pretty things to wear, and a big box pushed way under the lower boughs that Toddy opened last.

Olivia recalled the strange incident that happened next as they both watched Toddy tear away the wrappings and take off the lid of the box containing the big doll Helene had picked out for her "because, Grandmother, do you know Toddy has *never* had a real 'store-bought' doll?"

Slowly Toddy had lifted it out, exquisitely dressed with an angelic bisque face framed in long dark curls, and stared at it. Olivia exchanged a glance with Helene. This subdued reaction was not what they had expected. You would have thought a doll like that would have elicited cries of delight, that she would have been hugged and held and admired extravagantly. Instead, Toddy's face was expressionless and after a while she laid the doll gently back in its box, then turned to a colorful picture book about Holland.

Later, when Olivia had gone into Helene's bedroom to say good night, Helene registered her disappointment.

"I thought Toddy would adore the doll, Grandmother," she said, puzzled.

"Maybe we were mistaken, dear. Perhaps Toddy is too old for dolls."

It was a mystery to both of them. Neither could guess that at the sight of the beautiful doll, a phantom had crossed Toddy's heart. A scene flashed into her mind — that small painted face, with its pointed chin and huge dark-lashed eyes, brought a hurting memory painfully alive. The long-gone mother, the unfulfilled promise, and Mazel's parting words — "I'll bring you something nice back from Europe when I come, maybe a big French doll with real hair. You'd like that, wouldn't you?"

Toddy never played with the doll. It sat stiffly propped against the pillows of the window seat in her room, a silent reminder of a past growing dimmer but a hurt never healed.

January 1892
Mrs. Anna Scott
c/o The Rescuers and Providers Society

Dear Mrs. Scott,
Toddy has been with us now for nearly two years and we are very well pleased

with her progress, as I hope you will be.

She was promoted to the Fifth Grade, with A's and B's in all subjects, and is reported by her teacher, Miss Millicent Cady, to be attentive in class, diligent in studies, prompt with her homework. She is particularly fond of reciting and does well with oral reports and compositions.

Her disposition is consistently pleasant, her table and other manners much improved, and her overall demeanor is continually growing in refinement.

She is helpful and considerate in many ways around the house, not only in regard to Helene, my granddaughter, when she is unwell, but also is constantly finding ways she can be of assistance to me. She is generous and seems to find great pleasure in helping others.

As you know I had some reservations about taking Toddy as Helene's companion at first because she seemed altogether too lively and vivacious to be content in a life of a household necessarily centered on a semi-invalid child. But with each passing day I become more convinced we did find the "right home for the right child" as you and Mr. Scott said was your goal.

Sincerely,
Olivia Hale

January 1893
Mrs. Anna Scott
c/o The Rescuers and Providers Society

Dear Mrs. Scott,
It is hard to believe that another year has passed and that I am again sending you the required annual report on Toddy. She is so much a part of our household now that it is difficult to remember when she was not here. As my granddaughter remarked not too long ago, "Grandmother, wasn't our life boring before Toddy came?"

Indeed, I do not know what my granddaughter's life would be like now without the companionship of this child. Her life, I am much afraid, would have been not only boring but without much joy and very lonely. Deprived as she has been of the natural childhood environment of school, companions her own age, and the normal diversions and activities of a healthy girl, Toddy has been a real godsend to Helene. She brings her vibrant health, vivacious personality, her many activities into the sickroom to share with Helene. Even our doctor has remarked on the beneficial effect this has had on his patient.

By the above, I would not lead you to believe that Toddy's life is absolutely subverted to that of Helene's invalidism. Toddy has her own friends, regular outdoor exercise (this winter she learned to ice-skate and has gone sledding with her school friends), and is active in all sorts of events in both school and church. I just wanted you to know that her devotion to Helene is remarkable and I believe they really do consider each other "sisters."

Again, I must commend you and your husband for the marvelous work you continue to do in finding homes for these unfortunate children who, through no fault of their own, are left homeless. It is my sincere hope that other families who open their homes to one of these will be as satisfied as we have been.

Cordially,
Olivia Hale

January 1894
Mrs. Anna Scott
c/o The Rescuers and Providers Society

Dear Mrs. Scott,
I hope your trip to the Holy Land this fall was both edifying and enjoyable. Both the girls enjoyed the postcards you sent them and talked of nothing else for days but that one day, when Toddy was finished school and if Helene's health permitted, they, too, might make such a pilgrimage.

Speaking of Helene's health, we have both good and bad reports to make. She was feeling strong enough this summer for me to take the girls for a few weeks' stay at the seashore, hoping the mild climate and bracing ocean air would be beneficial. It did so seem and for weeks after our return, she seemed much stronger.

Unfortunately in the beginning of winter, she caught a bad cold which developed into pleurisy, and we were all quite anxious about her recovery. I must tell you, Toddy was a devoted nurse to her during her illness (provoking the very vocal complaints of the obsequious Miss Tuttle, I must add with some amusement). However, Helene seemed to quite prefer Toddy's ministrations to the aforementioned, which makes me wonder if perhaps Toddy has a talent in that direction and if we should encourage her to take training when she completes her high school education.

She also did a very nice recitation at the school Christmas program this year. She is growing into a very pretty young woman, delicate-boned, graceful and with a spritely charm.

From all this, you will gather we are a very content household and continue daily to be grateful to your society for placing Toddy with us. Enclosed you will find a check for a donation that will show my gratitude for the fine work you are doing in bringing the Orphan Trains west.

> With all good wishes to you and your husband, I am,
> Olivia Hale

12

"Grandmother, I want to give Toddy a birthday party," Helene began. "You see, she's never had one. Not ever. And she'll be thirteen and that's a very important age, don't you think? I mean, once you're into your teens, no one considers you a little girl anymore. It's a special birthday and I want to make it special for Toddy."

May sunshine flowed in through the windows of the dining room where Olivia and Helene were having breakfast alone, since Toddy had already left for school.

"I'd like it to be a surprise party. We could keep everything secret until the last minute. What do you think? Please say yes, Grandmother."

Mrs. Hale carefully buttered her toast before replying. Could it actually be *five* years since Toddy had come to live with them? Good heavens, how quickly the time had passed, she thought, giving an imperceptible shake of her head.

Helene, watching her grandmother closely, mistook that as a sign her request was being refused. Disappointed, she tried again. "I promise I won't overdo and Clara will help me. Won't you change your mind, Grandmother?"

"Change my mind?" Mrs. Hale exclaimed. Then a hint of a smile softened her expression as she realized Helene had mistakenly anticipated a negative answer. "No! Indeed I'll not change it! I think giving Toddy a party is a splendid idea."

Helene blinked, then grinned in understanding. "Oh, thank you, Grandmother! I can't wait to see Toddy's face when we all yell 'Surprise'."

Helene had already planned the party in her mind and she quickly enlisted the housekeeper's help to bring it to reality. There were consultations with Cook to concoct the perfect menu. It would be a luncheon served in the garden, for the early June weather was sure to be pleasant. There would be chicken salad, and tiny sandwiches, a fruit mold, lemonade and a marvelous cake — Toddy's favorite, an elaborate German chocolate, which was also the cook's specialty.

No effort was spared to keep the whole thing a secret. Helene designed and painted lovely watercolor invitations to send out to six of Toddy's friends, which, of course, included Laurel and Kit. Along with the time and day, there was a strict admonition to keep the party a secret. It was to be a complete surprise for Toddy.

Busy with all the events of the last week of school, Toddy, usually so aware of everything going on around her, was preoccupied. She did not seem to notice conversations that came to an abrupt halt at her approach or stopped completely when she entered a room. Concentrating on the poem she was to recite in the closing program, Toddy, uncharacteristically, was oblivious to everything else.

On the morning of the party there was a conspiracy of silence in the Hale household. No one was to mention Toddy's birthday. At breakfast, Helene asked Toddy if she would go downtown and do a few errands for her. Toddy readily agreed. Helene told her there was a handiwork project she wanted to start, and Toddy was given a long list of miscellaneous items she needed. It was a list guaranteed to keep Toddy occupied and away from the house for at least an hour or two.

Meanwhile, the balloons would be blown up and strung around the gazebo where the party table and chairs would be set up and decorated, and the brightly wrapped birthday presents piled nearby. Her unexpected guests would arrive and be hidden in the garden until it was time to spring the surprise on Toddy.

Clara was to watch for Toddy and then alert everyone to quiet down and stay hidden until she sent Toddy out to the garden on some pretext. Then they could all jump from their hiding places and shout "Surprise! Happy Birthday!"

Helene's face was flushed and Mrs. Hale glanced anxiously at her as she fussed over the table, moving the centerpiece of fragrant roses, smoothing the pink tablecloth, or straightening one of the place cards in the small porcelain flower holders that were to be party "favors" for each guest to take home.

Miss Tuttle had complained several times during the weeks of planning that Helene was doing too much, getting too excited. Being hostess for this lively group of girls, she maintained, was dangerous for someone of such fragile health. But Mrs. Hale had put aside her own concern and withstood the nurse's protests.

"Let her enjoy herself, Miss Tuttle," she said firmly. "Helene doesn't get many chances like this. If she has to stay in bed tomorrow — well, so be it. I don't want this event spoiled for her by gloomy predictions that will only make her nervous."

Olivia hoped she wouldn't regret her directive. All her life Helene had had to listen to this sort of cautionary advice and walk on eggshells while everyone around her held her breath. Planning this party for Toddy had given Helene enormous pleasure, and Olivia was determined it wasn't going to be ruined for her.

Everything went according to plan and Toddy arrived home, a little breathless from hurrying, a little concerned because she had not been able to find all the items on Helene's list. Helene, of course, had made sure of that by adding some supplies which would almost certainly be unavailable.

When Toddy stopped to explain to Mrs. Hubbard why it had taken her so long and how she had not been able to find some of the things Helene wanted, Mrs. Hubbard shuttled her out to the garden, saying Helene wanted to see her the minute she got home.

As soon as Toddy stepped outside, she was greeted by shrieks of "Surprise!" and "Happy Birthday." Toddy's face was Helene's reward.

Mrs. Hale stood at the parlor window which overlooked the garden, watching the fun and festivity. At a sudden burst of laughter, she smiled. What a good time they were having. Helene had been right. It was a wonderful idea to give Toddy a surprise party for her thirteenth birthday.

My, how the years go, she sighed. If Toddy was thirteen, that meant Helene was nearly eighteen — an age to which she had not been expected to live. Mrs. Hale breathed a prayer of thanksgiving. Helene seemed so much stronger. Surely Toddy's coming had given her the will to live. At least she was more *alive,* happier since Toddy had become her "little sister."

"Excuse me, madam." Clara's voice interrupted Olivia's thoughts. She turned to see her housekeeper standing in the doorway, a strange expression on her face.

"Yes, what is it, Clara?"

"There's — well, ma'am, there's a *person* at the front who *insists* on seeing you."

"A *person?*" Olivia frowned. "What do you mean? What kind of person?"

Clara darted a quick look over her shoulder and started to say something more, but before she could do so, she was pushed aside by a gaudily dressed woman who walked past her and into the parlor.

"Mrs. Hale?"

Olivia glanced questioningly at Clara then back at this stranger who had ad-

141

dressed her in a husky voice. At first, she was most aware of the hat the creature was wearing — a plumed affair that looked as though it weighted down her head. Under its brim emerged masses of curls that could only be described as orange. Her outfit was cut in the latest style, but the material was cheap, the workmanship shoddy. She carried a parasol that she tapped as she set it down in front of her.

She was young, in her early thirties Olivia guessed, pretty in a coarse sort of way. Her features were nice enough, but her complexion was obviously heightened by a liberal use of cosmetics. She had a theatrical look, a flamboyance in both dress and manner that unconsciously repelled Olivia.

"You *are* Mrs. Olivia Hale?" the woman repeated.

"Yes," Olivia replied coldly and was about to ask, "And who are you?" when the woman placed both hands on the handle of the parasol, leaned forward on it and announced, "I'm Mazel Todd, Mrs. Hale, and I've come to get my daughter."

These startling words, spoken in an exaggerated imitation of an upper-class English accent, sent a chill racing through Olivia's body. She felt every muscle in her body stiffen as she stared back at the woman.

To gain time, she let her gaze sweep from the quivering feathers on the astonishing hat down to the pointed toes of the high-heeled boots. All the time her mind was racing; she tried to gather her wits about her enough to absorb what the woman had said and deal with this unexpected, but dreadful turn of events.

The eyes of the two women were locked. It was Mazel who blinked first and glanced away. She had expected something, anything rather than this stony silence. She shifted her feet, then twisted the long, sleazy silk gloves she was carrying and fiddled with her beaded purse as she glanced around.

She did not miss a thing worth taking note of — the polished mahogany furniture, the crystal candlesticks on the mantelpiece with their glittering prisms, the marble-top tables and velvet upholstery. Her survey seemed to stiffen her posture.

"Is she here? My little girl, Toddy?"

Mrs. Hale gestured to one of the fan-backed armchairs.

"Won't you sit down, Mrs. — Todd."

Mazel hesitated a second then minced across the deep-piled carpet to the chair Mrs. Hale indicated. As she passed, Olivia thought she detected, in addition to a heavy scent of perfume, a whiff of something suspiciously alcoholic.

With a swish of her skirt, Mazel perched on the edge of the chair.

All Olivia's instincts tensed for battle. She felt certain this sudden, unexpected appearance meant trouble. What kind Olivia wasn't sure but, like an experienced soldier, she braced herself for combat.

She waited for the woman to speak, but Mazel was preoccupied, her eyes roaming greedily around, appraising everything. Olivia was forced to open the conversation.

"May I inquire how you happened to come here, Mrs. Todd?" Olivia asked. "And what is the purpose of your visit?"

"I told you. I come for my kid, that's what!" Mazel retorted, immediately on the defensive, her affected accent gone.

"But, Toddy lives *here* now. I adopted her, Mrs. Todd. I signed papers from the Rescuers and Providers Society who brought the children from Greystone Orphanage west by train for placement."

Mazel's face flushed.

"Them people had no right to do that. I didn't give them no permission for her to be adopted!"

"Surely, you understood when you left her at Greystone that children left over six months are made available for adoption?"

"I don't remember any such thing," Mazel snapped. "How did I know our troupe would get another engagement to tour the provinces in England? Then after that we went all over the Continent. We was billed as headliners in theaters in Germany and Austria. We had posters in five different languages sayin' we'd played before the crowned heads of Europe, we did." She preened herself, then added, "But I never expected to be gone this long."

"You've just returned from a — European — engagement, then?" Olivia asked.

Mazel's flush deepened. "Well, no, not *just*. I mean, we got back but we went on the road again right away and —"

"You must have checked with Greystone as soon as you returned to the States to see about Toddy, didn't you?"

Mazel shifted uneasily. "Well, not right away. I knew, I mean, I *assumed* she was safe and well took care of there and —" Mazel opened her purse and with a flourish pulled out a hanky dripping with lace, and dabbed her eyes. "And then when I come to get my baby girl, they told me she was gone!"

"Seven years later?" Olivia's voice emphasized the irony of this statement as she raised skeptical eyebrows.

Defiant, Mazel lifted her chin. She put

the handkerchief away and glared at Olivia.

Olivia ignored the look and pressed on.

"I understand Toddy was only six when she was brought to Greystone. Didn't it occur to you that she *might* be put up for placement if you didn't come back for her within six months? You *had* to have signed release forms with that stipulation when you left her at Greystone in the first place," Olivia persisted.

"I don't recall signin' no such thing!"

"You *did* sign such a paper though, Mrs. Todd. I *have* such a paper with your signature on it," Olivia replied evenly.

"I don't believe it! Where?"

"In my safe deposit box at the bank. Along with the other papers I myself signed."

Mazel dropped her eyes, started to fidget with the chain on her purse, knotting it, then unknotting it.

"How did you find out where Toddy was?" persisted Mrs. Hale.

"I run into an old friend who knew about the Orphan Trains. They keep records, you know."

"But Greystone is clear across the country, in Massachusetts. You mean to say you traveled all this way to get Toddy? Where do you live, Mrs. Todd? Where is the home you're going to give Toddy located?"

Under the rouge Mazel's face reddened again. "What do you mean?"

"Just what I asked. If you propose to take Toddy away from this comfortable home, where do you plan to live? Where is she to go to school? She's very bright, you know. In another year she'll start high school." Mrs. Hale's voice was very matter-of-fact.

Mazel looked flustered. When she didn't reply right away, Olivia followed up with another question.

"How did you happen to come here to Meadowridge, Mrs. Todd? It isn't exactly on the main road from Boston." A definite tinge of sarcasm was evident in Olivia's tone. Observing Mazel's discomfiture, Olivia pressed her advantage, her words clipped and sharp. "Do you want to hear what I believe is the truth, Mrs. Todd? I think somehow your . . . *profession* brought you into the vicinity. And somehow, I'm not quite sure how, you found yourself near where you learned your child had been placed. But —" here Olivia paused significantly — "I don't think you had any intention of coming to take Toddy until you learned who had adopted her . . . and saw this house."

Mazel's eyes widened. She looked startled, then a little frightened. Olivia knew she had called the woman's bluff. Somewhere in the back of her mind, she remembered seeing an ad in the newspaper about a dance troupe being part of the midway entertainment at the County Fair at Minersville, the next town over. That was *it!* After having found out where Toddy had been sent, Mazel must have known she was close enough to check it out. A few pertinent questions would have given her the address of the Hale mansion, plus the information that Olivia Hale was the wealthiest woman in town.

Trusting her intuition, Olivia prodded. "I think your curiosity brought you here, Mrs. Todd. And maybe a little greed. I think somehow you've done some investigating and discovered Toddy is my granddaughter's companion and very important to her. I believe you thought if you could come here and threaten to take her away, I would offer you some financial compensation for not doing so."

"Why, why —" Mazel sputtered. "That's insulting!"

"I believe it's true," Olivia declared quietly. "But, I also feel children should be with their natural parents whenever that is possible. And since you have come such a long way, and gone to so much trouble to find her — you must now be able to provide for her adequately." Olivia watched Mazel shrewdly, noticing her instant agitation. "I think we should let Toddy decide for herself."

"But, but —" began Mazel.

"She is outside in the garden with her friends. They're having a party. You know, *of course,* what day it is?" Olivia's eyes held hers in an unwavering gaze.

Mazel's mouth twitched in a nervous smile. "Oh, sure, I come by the school and seen it was closed. It's the start of summer vacation, right?"

Olivia did not bother to reply. Inwardly outraged that the woman didn't even remember it was her own child's birthday, she asked, "Shall I call Toddy in now, let her choose?"

Mazel jumped up. "Oh, I don't want to take her away from her friends." She paled under the garish makeup. Her hands fluttered, wringing the handkerchief. "Goodness knows if the kid would even remember me . . . it's been so long —" Her voice trailed away weakly as if she knew she had trapped herself by her own words.

"Hoist with her own petard," Mrs. Hale quoted to herself with grim satisfaction.

"So, Mrs. Todd, what do you propose to do now?" Olivia rose to her feet also.

"Well, I didn't mean to upset everybody." She shrugged, saying uneasily, "You're right. I don't have a proper home for a kid — a growin' young girl, I mean. We're tourin' all over the state, doin' the Fairs and then we're on to 'Frisco. California, you see. The company don't pay for families to travel with the dancers — I mean, it wouldn't be no life for a kid," she floundered.

"It's up to you, Mrs. Todd. Do you want to see Toddy? Take her with you?"

Mazel was panic-stricken. Her plans had collapsed. She was caught by this steely-eyed woman like a hooked fish on a line. Mentally, she flogged the friend who had egged her on to come here once she found out Toddy had been "placed out" with the wealthy Olivia Hale. She wished she'd never bothered that woman at the Rescuers and Providers Society with her story, putting on that act about being so shocked to find Toddy gone, so that the woman had broken the rules and given Mazel the Hale address, happy at the prospect of mother and daughter being reunited. They were both wrong.

Shamefaced, Mazel mumbled, "I guess —

I want to do what's best for her — the kid — for Toddy."

"Then, let us agree on it." Olivia unclenched the hands she had unconsciously been gripping so tightly in her lap during this interview. She walked over to her desk. "If you will sign a written statement that you will not try to contact me or Toddy in any way until she is eighteen, I shall write a check to cover all your expenses in coming here." She slid a piece of her expensive monogrammed stationery onto the blotter, picked up her pen, dipped it in the inkwell. Her quick, firm handwriting quickly covered the page with a few strong, clear sentences; then she beckoned Mazel over.

After Mazel had signed it, Olivia sat down and wrote out a check, folded it and handed it to Mazel, who hastily slipped it into her purse as if Olivia might snatch it back.

"Good afternoon then, Mrs. Todd." Rising and moving to the parlor door, Olivia held it open. Mazel scurried out without glancing at her hostess.

The same stern-faced, gray-haired woman who had let her in the house earlier was standing just outside the door in the hall and, without a word, opened the front door for her to exit.

On the front porch Mazel took out the

check, unfolded it and gasped. The sum was far more than she had ever expected! Maybe she should have been a little tougher, prolonged the suspense, made the old lady dig a little deeper.

Just then she heard the sound of girlish voices, a peal of laughter from around the side of the house. Mazel's curiosity got the better of her, and she went down the porch steps and walked around the house, her French heels teetering in the velvety soft grass. A high ornamental fence enclosed a formal garden. Mazel moved closer, peeking through the railings.

In the white-latticed gazebo she could see about a half-dozen young girls, dressed in pastel-colored dresses, gathered around a table, beautifully decorated with pink streamers and flowers, and piled high with brightly wrapped presents. They all seemed to be laughing and talking at the same time.

Which one was Toddy? Mazel wondered, pressing her face closer holding on to the iron posts. There was an older girl, slender, fragile-looking, the only one whose hair was worn up, who seemed to be in charge of things. Then there was another smaller one, with flyaway reddish-gold hair, moving like quicksilver. There was something about that one —

Johnny Todd! That same lightening grace, those dancing steps! That's *her!* Mazel's grip on the railings tightened. Something unfamiliar was squeezing her chest, making it hard to breathe.

Then Mazel shrugged and turned away. The kid had a good life. Why should she feel guilty? She'd probably done her a favor leaving her at Greystone.

In the parlor Olivia sank slowly into the sofa. She was trembling, and her heart was beating erratically. She was far too old for this kind of tension. What a brazen piece that woman was. Thank God, she'd been able to read her mind, to see through her trickery. Thank God, she had the money. If she hadn't, would Mazel have carried it off? Taken Toddy with her, introduced her to the shoddy, backstage life she herself was living? As pretty and talented as Toddy was, an unscrupulous stage manager might see the possibilities in her —

Olivia closed her eyes, drew a suddenly shaky hand across her brow, and took a deep breath.

A discreet knock on the door was followed by Clara herself, bringing a small tray.

"I thought you could do with a spot of tea,

ma'am," she said, putting it down on the table in front of Mrs. Hale.

The two women exchanged a wordless look. It was enough.

Then Clara stepped back, folded her arms, and with a nod toward the windows said, "The girls are havin' the time of their lives. And if I may say so, ma'am, sendin' that woman packin' is probably the best birthday present Toddy's ever had!"

13

The Class of 1900

The afternoon sun was sending long shadows across the grass as the four tennis players, having finished their set, prepared to go home. Tying the strings on her racket cover, Toddy shook back her hair impatiently. Her face was flushed from the exercise, and a few new golden freckles spattered her pert nose.

Beside her, Chris pulled a white, V-necked, cable-stitch sweater over his dark, tousled head.

Laurel and Dan, on the other side of the court, were talking in low tones when Toddy called to them. "Coming, you two?"

Dan picked up both their rackets. "Coming."

They joined Toddy and Chris at the gate of the tennis court and the four of them walked across the wide expanse of lawn in front of Meadowridge High.

"Has anyone done the final book report yet?" Toddy asked.

Chris moaned. "Ugh, don't mention it. *Ivanhoe*! So dull."

"Dull?" echoed Laurel. "I thought it was wonderful, so romantic!"

"Then maybe you can help me write a two-thousand-word theme on it," suggested Chris, looking hopeful. "I keep getting the characters mixed up, can't keep track of what's going on."

"Chris! Do your own work!" Toddy reproached him. "Why do you always expect other people to rescue you?"

"*Rescue?* You mean like a gallant knight rescuing the fair damsel from the tower of the wicked king?" he retorted, striking a dramatic pose with one arm held against his forehead.

"No! I didn't mean *that!* Not unless you consider yourself a damsel in distress!" she retorted. "But you do act like a young prince sometimes! I've seen you trying to wheedle someone into doing something for you that you're too lazy to do yourself — for example, make yourself read something you don't particularly like."

"Well, what's wrong with getting some help from a friend? If Laurel enjoys *Ivanhoe,* maybe she'd like to tell me about it and then I can write my report from *her* report!" argued Chris.

"It's not right! It would be better to turn in a report telling *why* you *didn't* like

Ivanhoe than give a second-hand version of someone else's report," she explained as if talking to a two-year-old.

"And get an 'F'? When everyone knows Mrs. Harrison *adores* Sir Walter Scott and everything he writes?" countered Chris.

"At least he knows who wrote *Ivanhoe*," Dan intervened, laughing.

"Thanks, my friend," Chris said. "See, Dan knows you're falsely accusing me of dishonorable motives."

"You men! You always stick together!" declared Toddy.

"Why not? You girls certainly do. Toddy, Laurel and Kit — the invincible, insepa-rable trio —"

"You're deliberately changing the sub-ject," Toddy said severely. "We were talking about how you always expect spe-cial treatment. Like royalty! The Prince of Hemlock Hill." She made an exaggerated sweeping bow. "What is your highness's pleasure? How can we serve you, O Prince?"

"*You* should talk! It's the Hale house that looks like a castle, not my humble abode, even if it is on Hemlock Hill," Chris snapped back.

Dan and Laurel exchanged glances. They were used to the way Toddy and Chris baited each other.

"But I'm only a lowly servant, not the Crown Prince of the royal house of Blanchard!" jeered Toddy, her blue eyes twinkling.

Though he knew she was teasing, Chris colored under his tan, and Toddy, realizing she might have gone a little too far, eyed him warily. Then, as he made a snatch for her hair ribbon, she dodged and started to run. Chris took off after her.

Even though he was a natural athlete, Toddy was small and light and very fast. She whisked through the iron gate of the Hales' impressive Victorian home and shut it. Breathless and laughing, she leaned over the gate as he came panting up on the other side.

"Tortoise!" she teased.

"Don't you ever let up?" he scowled.

"Not when you're such an easy target!"

A worried expression crossed Chris's handsome boyish face and he asked, "Toddy, you don't really think I'm — well, all you said, do you?"

She put her head to one side as if studying him intently.

"Well, only a little —" The dimples on either side of her rosy mouth winked. "You know you wouldn't *object* if Laurel, or better still, *Kit,* would write your book report for you, now be honest, would you?"

"Come on!" Chris was derisive. "Even *you* might be tempted to have *Kit* write something for you!"

"I do my *own* work! I might not be the best student, but I respect *integrity,* even if it means getting a low grade."

Chris looked skeptical. "Toddy —" he began.

"Oh, well —" she pursed her lips in contemplation. "I'll admit it would be *tempting* — Everyone knows Kit's the writer in the class. But that's not the point!"

"Now, take back the rest of what you said," Chris demanded.

"I don't remember what I said —"

"You know the part I mean, about my being the 'Prince of Hemlock Hill'," Chris insisted.

"Oh, *that!*"

"Yes, *that!*"

"I must have hit a nerve, if you're so upset about it!" Toddy taunted.

"Come on, Toddy."

"But, *that* part *is* true, Chris. You know it is. Your mother spoils you silly!"

Chris knew there was *some* truth to that and decided not to deny it. Instead, he changed the subject. "Did I tell you my father is taking me up to the University the week after graduation? There's some kind of alumni weekend, a father-son sort of thing. He wants to introduce me to the right people up there in case I don't get an athletic scholarship or in case my grades aren't acceptable."

"Oh, you'll get in, Chris, no question." Although she didn't say so, Toddy felt sure Mr. Blanchard had pulled enough strings to ensure his son's acceptance into the University he was so proud to have graduated from himself. He'd do it, no matter what it took — a sizable donation to the building fund or even a new building! Or preferably a gymnasium or basketball court where Chris could star.

"I don't know exactly how I feel about going to the University when it comes right down to it," Chris said slowly. "I don't like the idea of going so far from Meadowridge, for one thing. I mean, I guess it will be interesting and the sports stuff will be fun, but —" Chris stopped mid-sentence. The words he was fumbling to say left him — escaped in his sudden realization of how pretty Toddy was.

Funny, he'd never noticed before. She's always been, well — just *Toddy*. Now he gave her a sidelong appraisal. In the slant of

160

the setting sun, her red-gold hair flamed to life, curling fetchingly about her pixyish face. The lithe, neat figure fairly burst with energy. But it was her eyes that held him — sparkling, always hinting of mischief and what was that French phrase? *joie de vivre!* He grinned. Wouldn't she be impressed to know he could come up with *that?*

"What's the matter?" Toddy prodded. "Are you afraid of being homesick?"

"No! It's not that," Chris said indignantly, coming out of his reverie. "It's just that it will be a long way to come — I mean, I'll miss seeing you, Toddy."

Toddy seemed pleasantly surprised, but her tone was amused. "They let you out for holidays and good behavior, don't they?"

"Doggone it, Toddy, aren't you ever serious?" Chris said, losing his temper. He leaned over the gate and yanked off her hair ribbon. She made a futile grab for it but Chris was already backing away.

"So long! See you tomorrow!" he called over his shoulder, and trotted down the street toward Hemlock Hill.

"I'll get you for this, Chris Blanchard, see if I don't!" Toddy shouted after him. But all she heard was laughter as he turned the corner.

She shook back her hair, now tumbling all

around her shoulders in a riot of ringlets and started up the path to the house. She just reached the bottom step when the front door opened and Mrs. Hubbard, the housekeeper, stood there, glaring.

"What gets into you, I'd like to know? Carrying on like a regular hoyden with that Blanchard boy right out in front of the house! And look at you, hair every whichaway, shirtwaist coming out of your skirt! Tsk, tsk!" Clara Hubbard shook her head in despair. "Come along inside. Miss Helene's been wondering about you, said she was supposed to help you study for your history exam tomorrow!"

"I almost forgot, sorry!" Toddy murmured as she skipped past the disapproving bulk of the housekeeper and sprinted up the wide staircase, calling as she went, "I'm coming, Helene. Sorry I'm late!"

Nearing the top of Hemlock Hill, Chris slowed to a trot as the large, gray house his mother always referred to as "our Queen Anne" came into view. Chris winced. Maybe Toddy was right. Sometimes his mother *did* put on airs. It made him squirm to think of it.

Maybe it was just because she was proud of being the wife of the president of

Meadowridge Bank, the *only* bank in town. But that didn't make them "royalty" or make *him* a "prince"!

He halted and looked at Toddy's hair ribbon still in his hand. Rolling it up, he jammed it into the pocket of his tennis flannels and walked slowly toward home.

Chris wished his mother wasn't always pushing him to ask other girls out, accept invitations to parties given by people he didn't care anything about. He didn't want to be with anyone but Toddy. Compared to her, other girls seemed so ordinary.

Well, he would be taking Toddy to the Class Picnic and the Awards Banquet and most certainly to the dance on graduation night! No matter what his mother said!

14

The sunlight on Toddy's hair fired it with dancing sparks of red and gold. Though tied back with a broad, dark blue ribbon, clusters of ringlets had managed to escape and curled in tight tendrils over her forehead and around her ears.

Chris, gazing at her across the table at the Senior Class Picnic, thought she looked especially nifty today in her trim blue-checked shirtwaist and darker blue chambray shirt, her tiny waist nipped in with a wide belt.

They had all lunched heartily on cold fried chicken, potato salad, several kinds of homemade pies and cakes, as well as fresh-cut watermelon at three of the long rustic tables pushed into a U-shape for more conviviality.

The small class of seniors who had grown close during the past four years were a congenial group. There was a great deal of boisterous laughter, good-natured teasing and jokes during the meal. When they finished there was still the rest of the afternoon ahead, and they began to break up into smaller groups to wander along the winding paths of the big park.

Chris suggested to Toddy that they walk up to the bluff overlooking the river, and she invited Laurel and Dan to come along.

Much to Toddy's irritation, Chris continued an argument that had been interrupted by lunch.

"But I don't see why I can't take you to the Awards Banquet, Toddy."

"I've already told you, Chris. Helene and Mrs. Hale are coming and I'll be with them."

"But the seniors are going to have their own table. Doesn't your family know you'll be sitting with your class?"

"Of course, they know *that,* Chris. And I'll see you there and sit with you then. But Helene is so excited about all the graduation events, and I do so want her to feel a part of everything I'm doing."

"But being with your class is important. It will be the last time we'll all be together as a class. Can't Helene understand that?" he persisted.

"How *could* she, Chris? Helene's never had a chance to go to a real school, be a part of a real class. I'm just trying to give her the feeling that this is her graduation, too. It means so much to her, don't you see that?"

"Well, what about afterwards? You know Mother wants to give our class a party after the Banquet. You can go with me to that, can't you?"

"Oh, Chris, I don't know. I'm not sure."

"What do you mean 'not sure'?" Chris sounded shocked.

"I think, I mean, I'm almost sure, Mrs. Hale has planned some kind of surprise for me after the Awards —" Toddy felt guilty at Chris's crestfallen expression.

"I don't believe this!" he exclaimed. "I told you about this party weeks ago! There just won't be any party if you're not there. Why would I even want to have a party if you aren't coming! It was Mother's idea anyway. I'll just call it off," he declared.

"Oh, you can't do that, Chris!" protested Toddy. "Your mother would be so upset, and she'd be furious at me for being the cause of it."

"Then promise you'll work it out with Mrs. Hale and Helene," he said stubbornly.

"How am I supposed to do that? Ask them if they are planning a surprise for me? I can't do that."

"Hey, you two. Stop arguing!" called Dan from the top of the hill. "It's too nice a day for quarreling."

Toddy grinned. "He's right. Come on, let's go down to the river," she said and held out her hand.

Chris, still angry, hesitated for a second, but Toddy was smiling at him appealingly. And in this mood, Toddy was hard to resist. He could never stay mad at her long. With a sigh, Chris gave in, took her hand and together they started down the path to the river.

Toddy balanced herself delicately as she hopped from rock to rock along the edge of the river. Chris followed with longer, surer strides. For the moment they had ended their verbal sparring and were simply enjoying the easy companionship they had known since they were both children. All of a sudden Toddy, one foot poised behind the other, seemed to wobble precariously.

"Whoops!" she cried and Chris reached out, putting both his hands around her waist to steady her. He held her until she regained her footing. She paused, then stuck one foot out tentatively to the next rock.

"I'm all right, now. You can let go!" she told him.

Chris's hands remained a split second longer, then released her. She ran ahead with a few light steps. Making it to the strip of sand, she turned and smiled as he came alongside her.

There's something different about Chris, Toddy thought. *Wonder what it is.* She looked at him more closely. He was tall and tan, with the most amazing blue eyes. And he had that lopsided grin revealing teeth, straight and white and square. Her heart did a queer little flutter.

Why? What had come over her? She'd known Chris forever, or almost forever, at least since she had come to live in Meadowridge nearly ten years ago. He was the first person her own age she had met. They had climbed trees together, had gone through school together. Except for Kit and Laurel, Toddy had always thought of Chris as her closest friend. So why this new unsettling feeling, this new awareness of him?

Toddy found her mind hurtling back through the years, seeing them like the picture cards in Helene's steriopticon set, remembering Chris as the teasing tormentor of grammar school days, when he had been afraid to acknowledge their friendship in front of his jeering boyfriends at school, tweaking her hair ribbons, chasing her on the playground. But when they reached high school, a different pattern emerged.

Chris soon became the most popular boy at Meadowridge High. A handsome six feet, with a powerful athletic build, easygoing and likable, he was a champion runner and the star of the basketball team. All the girls admired him, secretly longed for his attention. Wary of his new popularity, Toddy had kept her distance when they entered the new school. But at the beginning of their junior year, it was Toddy Chris began to seek out.

At first Toddy wondered about this new grown-up Chris, wondered if his looks were all he had going for him and if he had become dull as paint and conceited to boot. But she soon discovered under the aloof facade the little-boy "pal" still existed. After that they were friends again and any social activity that required a partner usually found them together.

Not that Toddy had no other choice. Vivacious and outgoing, Toddy, too, was popular. The same personality skills that Toddy had perfected to win acceptance and affection within the Hale household were applied with other people as well. If she was cheerful and friendly to everyone, she expected everyone to like her in return. If she ever suspected her popularity earned her detractors, who made snide remarks behind her back, Toddy pretended she did not know. She had learned long ago, the hard way, that to survive there were some things you had to overlook. One thing she knew for sure, she would never do anything to jeopardize her hard-won place with the Hales.

She and Chris walked slowly now along the riverbank, under the graceful swaying branches of the willows. There seemed to be an almost sleepy haze over everything — the afternoon sunlight dappling the water, making it glitter as it flowed over the rocks and swirled into the eddies.

How many times had they walked together like this? Yet this day had a different, indescribable quality, as though it were detached somehow from all the rest of the days they had ever been together. They weren't even arguing about anything, or teasing each other.

Then Chris took her hand, and Toddy looked up into those blue eyes. They stopped walking, as if startled by the contact of palm against palm. The unspoken words between them remained unsaid. It was as if neither wanted to spoil this strangely special moment.

Toddy felt a gathering tension she could not name or explain. She withdrew her hand and moved a little ahead to gather some of the wildflowers — Queen Anne's lace and purple lupin — making a little nosegay.

"I'll take these home to Helene," she said. Helene rarely had a day like this to enjoy.

"Wildflowers don't last long," Chris remarked.

"She'll enjoy them this evening anyway," Toddy replied, thinking days like this didn't last either. The breeze off the river was turning cool and the afternoon was nearly over. "I guess we'd better go back to the others," she suggested and with her hands full of flowers, Chris couldn't hold one hand as they clambered back up the hill to the high meadow.

15

As Toddy arrived for the Awards Banquet with Helene and Mrs. Hale, she saw that the high school gymnasium had been turned into a banquet hall. Tables had been set up all around the room, with one T-shaped one in the middle reserved for Mr. Henson, the principal, and such dignitaries as Mayor Thompson, the County Superintendent of Schools.

The table for the Senior Class extended from the head table and was decorated in the class colors. It was draped with twisted streamers of green and gold crepe paper, with great bunches of yellow daffodils, centered in wreaths of green leaves and flanked by tall gold candles, set at intervals down its length. Marking each senior's place was a rosette of gold and green satin ribbon with CLASS OF 1900 in sparkly gold letters to pin on a coat lapel or the shoulder of a dress.

Toddy waved to a few of her friends, then escorted Helene and Mrs. Hale, regal in black lace and pearls, to one of the tables reserved for the families of the graduates. Helene, who had rested all afternoon so she would be able to attend, wore a lovely apricot taffeta dress that lent color to her pale face and skillfully disguised her frail form.

As Toddy seated them with the parents of one of her classmates, she said regretfully to Helene, "I wish I could sit with you, tell you who everyone is, but the seniors all have to be together."

"Of course, Toddy. I understand. You go on and be with your friends," Helene reassured her. "Grandmother and I will be fine."

Toddy wasn't too sure when she left and looked back over her shoulder to see the chatty Mrs. Burroughs animatedly introducing herself to Mrs. Hale. Well, maybe it would do her good to mix with other people more — at least for one night. She kept herself too isolated up in the house on the hill. And Helene, of course, was too cloistered. Toddy wished there was something she could do to bring Helene into a more normal flow of activity. But everyone in the household was always so concerned about Helene's health that it was impossible to overcome all the objections to some of the outings Toddy suggested. Sometimes she felt frustrated trying. She *did* invite her own friends often and Helene always seemed to enjoy them.

Toddy wondered if all the fuss over her heart condition didn't make Helene too conscious of it. If they would just let her *do* something sometime without all the planning and preparation, the insistence on rest before and after, and having Dr. Woodward come at the least little flutter or fever. Was Helene *really* that fragile?

When Toddy reached the Senior Table and was greeted enthusiastically by her fellow classmates, her troubling thoughts about Helene disappeared. Chris had saved a place for her, with Laurel and Kit sitting opposite. For the moment she lost herself in lively conversation.

A chicken dinner was followed by fresh peach ice cream and little cakes iced in green and gold frosting. Then Mr. Henson rose, tapped on his water glass with his fork, and gradually the hum of conversation subsided until it was only a murmur before quieting completely.

"Ladies and gentlemen, parents, friends, and our honored guests, the Class of 1900!" Mr. Henson smiled with benevolence — an attitude with which he had not *always* regarded those particular young men and women. "Tonight we are here to honor several students with special awards which they have earned by outstanding work, talent, or skill. But before we begin our award ceremony, we have a treat in store — a musical rendition by one of our own. Many of you have enjoyed hearing her in the church choir or on other occasions. We now present Laurel Woodward."

Only Toddy and Kit noticed the sudden rush of color into Laurel's face at this introduction. "Laurel *Woodward.*" They had all discussed the problem many times when the three of them were alone together.

In spite of the fact that the Woodwards had legally adopted her, Laurel had stubbornly insisted on retaining her birth name, Laurel Vestal, and used it on all her copybooks and school papers until Miss Cady had taken her aside the day she was promoted out of the eighth grade.

"Laurel, next year you will be entering high school, and I suggest you begin using the name 'Laurel Woodward.' You know Dr. and Mrs. Woodward have officially changed your name to theirs. I think it hurts them when you don't use it."

So Laurel had given in. But somehow she still resented being forced to do so. In her own heart and mind she was *still* Laurel Vestal.

Laurel's voice rose sweetly — each note clear and true. When she finished, the room was hushed. Then slowly the clapping began and went on and on, even after Laurel returned to her place at the table, shaking all over.

Toddy whispered, "I think they expect an encore."

But Laurel just shook her head and finally the applause died away.

Then Mr. Henson was making another announcement. "And now we'll proceed with the presentation of the Awards. First, for his outstanding athletic ability in both Track and Basketball, the winner of four letters and the trophy for County Athlete of the Year, our own Chris Blanchard."

Toddy joined in the wild clapping as Chris, red-faced, went up to receive the engraved loving cup. He mumbled "Thank you." Then, clutching the trophy, he ambled back to the table, sank into his seat, and glanced at Toddy for approval.

Several other awards were announced. Dan won the Science Prize and Kit, the award for English Composition. Toddy's heart swelled with pride to see her two friends receiving tribute for work well done.

But when her own name was announced for the best dramatic performance of the year, Toddy could hardly believe her ears.

She had loved the role of Portia in *The*

Merchant of Venice, loved being part of the production, even memorizing her lines and the rehearsals. The night the play was given, she had donned her costume as though it belonged to her and moved out onto the stage with a minimum of stomach butter-flies.

Although she had joined the Drama Club her freshman year in high school, this year was the first Toddy had had the courage to try out for a part. Before, she had just volunteered to paint scenery, sell advertising for the program, help with costumes, or usher on opening night.

Toddy could not explain her reluctance, even to herself. There had seemed some inner denial of how desperately she wanted to get up on the stage and perform. In a way, the excitement she felt, the relish of ap-plause, seemed somehow unworthy, as if it were a vice rather than a virtue.

Or maybe, it was something far deeper. The last nine years had been so far removed from her early gypsy life of the vaudeville theater, that sometimes Toddy had the feeling it had never happened.

Several times, however, she had over-heard Miss Tuttle's comment to Mrs. Hub-bard when discussing some minor infraction. "Blood will tell," she had said

177

with a knowing look.

Had these years of affluence and respectability, living with the Hales, erased her true identity? Or was she, after all, still the child of a chorus girl and a roving song and dance man?

Yes, in a way, Toddy had felt there was something shameful about wanting to be in the play, loving doing it so much. But now she was being rewarded for it. Somehow Toddy got to her feet and managed to get up to the platform and make a nice little acceptance speech.

Olivia Hale, listening to Toddy expressing her thrill at winning the Drama Award, realized she was nervously pleating her napkin in her lap.

Zephronia Victorine Todd was now known as Toddy Hale. Only a few Meadowridge people remembered how she had arrived on the Orphan Train nearly ten years ago.

Olivia glanced at Helene, who was clapping her thin hands delightedly. She too was recalling the night they had attended the play together and heard Toddy say those memorable lines: "The quality of mercy is not strain'd, It droppeth as the gentle rain from heaven." Olivia herself could not remember ever being more moved by an acting performance.

Was Toddy a born actress? Would she leave someday, drawn by some inner compulsion to her parents' precarious profession? Those two irresponsible people who had abandoned her? Would "blood tell," after all?

And what would happen to Helene if Toddy followed this illusion, this dream Toddy herself might not yet recognize? Again, Olivia looked over at her granddaughter. Helene's delicate face was flushed. She looked so fragile tonight that it frightened Olivia.

At least she had been able to give Helene her heart's desire, a "little sister," whom she adored, she comforted herself. But was it right to expect Toddy to remain with Helene forever? Olivia recalled Dr. Woodward's comments a few years ago, "If Helene continues to receive the tender, loving care you are able to provide for her, if there is no stress or sudden shock, she could possibly live for many years. To be truthful, given the condition of her heart, I am gratified that she has survived this long."

Olivia was convinced having Toddy in their home had been a strong reason for Helene's continued well-being. But what if

Toddy left? And she herself could not live forever. What would become of Helene then?

At the next table sat the Blanchards. Bernice Blanchard's eyes were not on the recipient of the Drama Award so much as they were fixed speculatively on her son. It was plain to see that Chris could hardly contain his proud reaction to Toddy's triumph.

Bernice felt a mixture of irritation and concern. Why, oh why had her dear boy — such a catch — so stubbornly set his sights on that little nobody from nowhere? Chris, Bernice was positive, could have any girl in town. Why, there was a steady stream of invitations to parties, picnics, outings of all kinds from far more suitable girls, daughters of some of the best families in Meadowridge.

Not that Olivia Hale wasn't considered at the very top of Meadowridge society *if* she cared to participate in any of the social events. Now, if it had been *Olivia's granddaughter* Chris was interested in, that would be a different story! But, Helene, poor thing! Well, there was no use wasting time on the unavailable.

With narrowed eyes Bernice observed Toddy, looking undeniably charming in a white muslin dress embroidered all over with tiny daisies, and a wide, green sash spanning her tiny waist, her red-gold curls swirled up in a becoming style.

Well, thank goodness, in the fall Chris would be going away to the University and meeting lots of pretty girls. Bernice pursed her mouth petulantly. Perhaps in a few months in a new place with lots of new activities, Chris would get over his silly infatuation for Toddy.

Of course, Bernice sighed, there was still the long summer to get him safely through. And anything could happen in a summer!

16

Bright June sunlight poured in through the open windows of Toddy's bedroom, the breeze sending the ruffled curtains billowing like sails. She was putting the finishing touches on her hair when Helene tapped on the door, then stuck her head in.

"Need any help?" she asked.

"Oh, yes, Helene, will you please? The buttons on my right cuff! I can't seem to manage them with my left hand. Or maybe I'm just too nervous," she said with a little giggle.

"*You* nervous, Toddy. You who won the best actress award? Nothing to be nervous about. All you have to do is go up when they call your name and get your diploma!"

"That's just it. I can play Portia or somebody else. I'm not so sure when I'm being myself."

"You'll do fine, don't worry. And Grandmother and I will be there to give you moral support and clap our hands off when you stand up."

Toddy held out her arm for Helene to fasten the tiny pearl buttons.

"You look lovely, Toddy," Helene told her. "That dress is perfect."

Toddy twirled around, sending the white dotted Swiss skirt flaring.

Another tap came at the bedroom door at this point, and both girls turned as Mrs. Hale, carrying a small package bowed with silver ribbon, came in.

"Are you nearly ready, Toddy? I thought the graduates were supposed to be at school a half hour before the program starts. But then promptness was never your forte, was it." She spoke with a severity that seemed surprising on such a special day. "I do think you should learn to be on time from now on."

Toddy looked appropriately repentant. She knew tardiness was one of her besetting sins. It seemed that no matter how early she started to get ready to go somewhere, things got hectic at the last and she usually dashed out a few minutes behind schedule, leaving her drawers half opened and chaos in her wake.

"Yes ma'am, I'll try," said Toddy with suitable humility. Why was Helene smiling, she wondered? And Mrs. Hale's mouth was twitching.

"Maybe this will help." Olivia offered her the daintily wrapped package.

Toddy looked at her in surprise. Her pretty dress and white kid slippers with French heels were, she imagined, her graduation presents. Now something more?

"Well, go ahead, Toddy, open it!" urged Helene.

Toddy pulled the ribbons and paper to reveal a tiny leather box. Lifting its lid she saw an exquisite gold oval watch on a narrow, braided gold chain suspended from a delicate fleur-de-lis of gold and blue enamel.

"Do you like it?" Helene asked eagerly as Toddy stared speechlessly. "Here, let me pin it on for you."

"Oh, it's beautiful! Thank you! Thank you so much!" Her face was at once all smiles.

"Well, the jeweler set it for you, Toddy. So there's no excuse for you to be late to your own graduation — or anything else in the future!" said Mrs. Hale as she swept out of the room, a twinkle in her eye.

"Helene, I know you picked this out for me! It's the nicest thing I've ever had. Thank you!" She hugged Helene.

"Look out, Toddy. I'll wrinkle you!"

"I don't mind these kinds of wrinkles!" Toddy declared. "They're love wrinkles!" She laughed and Helene joined in.

"Oh, Toddy, I love you! What did we ever do without you?" sighed Helene.

Olivia Hale sat in one of the rows reserved for the parents and family of the graduates, with Helene beside her. One face stood out among all the eager young faces on the stage — a piquant, smiling face alert with intelligence.

"Zephronia Victorine Todd" would be written in fine calligraphy on her diploma. Olivia felt that familiar, vaguely disturbing sensation she had whenever she thought of those legal papers lying in her desk drawer. The adoption papers she had had drawn up after that shocking visit from Mazel Todd five years ago, but had never signed. Why not?

Helene had wanted her to legally adopt Toddy right away, but for some reason Mrs. Hale had put it off. She kept telling herself she wanted to see how things would work out. But before she had had her lawyer prepare the adoption document, that dreadful woman had arrived on her doorstep. Remembering that day, Toddy's thirteenth birthday, Olivia shuddered.

Well, she had paid the woman off, but would she be back? The payment was not that large, and there was no guarantee she

185

would not come back for more. All she had agreed to do was stay away until Toddy was eighteen. Well, Toddy had just turned eighteen.

Olivia also felt guilty that she had never told Toddy about her mother's visit, but she had not wanted to "rock the boat," as the saying went. She especially did not want to upset Helene, who loved Toddy like her own flesh and blood. Well, this was hardly the time to bring it up, Olivia thought.

She glanced at Helene sitting beside her. The chiseled profile seemed even sharper. Had she lost more weight? Olivia felt a little stirring of alarm, and she moved uneasily in her seat.

Perhaps they ought to go somewhere this summer, all three of them. Take Helene somewhere that would be a pleasant change of climate and scene. It could be a kind of graduation present for Toddy, too.

Yes, that might be the wise thing to do. Close the house and go. Then if that woman got any ideas about coming back into Toddy's life, making demands — they'd be far away.

Where would they go? Europe? Yes, that would be educational for both the girls. And they could make it a leisurely journey, no hurrying from country to country, city to city. Why, there was no reason to hurry. They could take months traveling, even a year —

They could even visit some of those health spas the Continent was so famous for, the ones in Austria and Switzerland. It might be exactly the thing for Helene.

Olivia settled back in her seat as that attractive, nice-looking young fellow came up to the podium. What was his name? Olivia referred to her program, ah, Daniel Brooke, Salutatorian. His was the welcoming address. She folded her hands in her lap, her expression composed. She would start making plans tomorrow for their trip. The girls would be delighted, she felt sure.

But Helene, ever sensitive to Toddy's desires, expressed and unexpressed, made a tactful suggestion. "I think, though she would never say so, that Toddy would really prefer to spend this summer at home, Grandmother. Some of her friends will be leaving in the fall and I'm sure she would like to be with them as much as possible."

So Olivia's plans were postponed, and in June the summer seemed to stretch endlessly before them. The freedom from the routine of school, classes, and homework was welcomed by casual students like

Toddy and Chris. There were weeks of unbroken sunny days to enjoy, mornings of tennis or bicycling out to the river to picnic and swim. Afternoons were spent playing croquet or badminton on someone's lawn, sipping lemonade under shady trees. The soft summer evenings offered twilight band concerts in the park, ice cream socials at the Community Hall, strolling home after the Sunday Youth Meeting at the church, gathering on porches or in parlors, around pianos singing.

It wasn't until after the Fourth of July that they realized that the time was fast approaching when many of the young people in their crowd would be going their separate ways.

Kit, of course, had been working full-time at the Library, as had Dan at Groves Pharmacy, both squirreling away what they earned to help with their college expenses. But even they had joined the others in the leisurely enjoyment of their last real summer together.

Then something happened that changed at least three of them.

The first Sunday in August, at the end of the church service, Reverend Brewster announced the arrival of a visiting evangelist who would conduct a Revival in Meadowridge. The Revival would begin on Wednesday and there would be meetings each evening for the rest of the week.

"Come prepared to receive a blessing," exhorted Reverend Brewster. "Don't let anything keep you home from these divine appointments."

Chris, who was waiting outside of church for Toddy, complained, "Wouldn't you know it would be the same week as the Carnival?"

Toddy looked shocked. "Shame on you, Chris Blanchard! Didn't you hear anything Reverend Brewster said? Not to let anything keep you from attending?"

Chris tried to look ashamed. "Then *you're* planning to go?" he asked.

"Of course!"

Chris glanced in the direction of Mrs. Hale and Helene who had walked on and were already seated in the open barouche, ready to drive home.

"I only meant — I mean, I was just going to see if you'd like to go to the Carnival with me," he said defensively. "It opens tomorrow. That's before the Revival even begins. They're already setting up over at the town park."

"I'll have to ask," she told him. "And if Mrs. Hale says I may, *and if* I decide to go, you have to promise to come to the Revival meetings," she said with satisfaction.

"I'll tell you all about the Carnival when I get home, Helene!" Toddy promised as she poked her head in the door of Helene's room the following evening. Helene, who was propped up in bed reading, put down her book and smiled.

"Have fun, Toddy. I'll see you later."

With a wave of her hand, Toddy flew down the stairs where an impatient Chris was trying to converse with Mrs. Hale.

"Have a good time, you two," she told them as they went out the door.

Chris tucked Toddy's hand through his arm as they started down the street. Over the tops of trees they could see the lights from the Carnival illuminating the lavender evening sky. The sound of the tinny calliope music from the merry-go-round swirled through the air, beckoning them with its own distinctive charm.

Hearing it, a strange little tingle of excitement quivered through Toddy, as if something familiar was triggered within her.

Approaching the entrance to the park, they experienced the smell of canvas and sawdust mingled with the sticky sweetness of cotton candy, the rich greasy aroma of popcorn, the strong odors of caravans and horses belonging to the performers tethered near the tents.

Chris held Toddy's hand as they meandered down the midway through the concession booths selling all kinds of garish wares, the barkers hoarsely enticing customers to "take a chance," "try your luck," "win your sweetheart a prize, mister."

They stopped at one so Chris could throw a few balls at a target, and astounded a chagrined concessionaire when he hit all three dead center. When the man tried to persuade Chris to try for another round, Toddy pulled him away, laughing at the man's sour expression as he parted grudgingly with Chris's "prize" — a gaudily painted plaster bulldog.

"Let's ride the Ferris wheel," Chris suggested and handed over a strip of tickets to the rough-looking operator with a cigarette dangling from one end of his mouth. He raised the safety bar and Toddy and Chris settled themselves in the flimsy seat. A minute later they were thrust swiftly back and upward into the night sky. Toddy gave a small cry of alarm and Chris put his arm protectively around the back of the seat. At the top, the Ferris wheel stopped with a jolt and they swung precariously, suspended over Meadowridge.

"Oh, my!" exclaimed Toddy with a nervous giggle.

"Scared?" Chris teased, purposely rocking their chair.

"Chris, don't!" she cried, clutching his arm.

He laughed indulgently.

"Don't worry. You're perfectly safe . . . with *me*." His arm dropped down on her shoulder and he leaned a little closer. "Toddy," he said tentatively. "Toddy, would you wear my class pin if I gave it to you before I leave for the University?"

Her heart jumped. Her sudden lightheadedness, she knew, had nothing to do with the dizzying height. Toddy did not answer for a minute.

"I don't know if that's a good idea, Chris," she replied at last. "You're going to be meeting lots of girls at college. Giving me your pin to wear is kind of . . . well, serious."

"Please, Toddy, I want you to have it. Going away isn't going to make any difference to me. I don't care how many pretty girls I meet." Chris stopped, then stammered. "You know, I — I love you, don't you?"

Just then the Ferris wheel started again with a jerk and they were whirled down and around again, leaving Toddy quite breathless. There was another quick spin and then they were brought to an abrupt stop, the safety bar was raised, and their ride was over.

"Think about it, won't you, Toddy?" Chris pleaded as they started walking toward the midway again.

As they passed one gaily striped tent three women dressed in orange, red and bright blue tinsel-trimmed dresses and wearing matching plumed hats came prancing out on a narrow stage, whirling their feather boas, while a thin, mustachioed man in a loud "Dapper Dan" yellow and green plaid suit and derby hat played the crowd.

"Come one, come all, ladies and gen'lmen, to see the Toast of Paree, the beauteous Trenton Threesome, rivaling the famed Flora Dora girls of the Zeigfield Follies, they've danced before the Crowned Heads of Europe! You ain't seen nothin' till you see these footsie-wootsies do their Spanish fandango! Jest fifty cents a head, folks. You can see what the continental nobility had to pay a fortune to view! Step right up, folks! Get your tickets right here!"

While they stopped to listen to his spiel, an icy finger trailed down Toddy's spine. Rooted to the spot, her eyes were riveted to the painted faces of the three dancers mincing on high-heeled boots across the stage, flouncing the ruffles of their fringed skirts to the music blaring from the brass funnel of a Gramophone inside the tent.

Her stomach lurched sickeningly and, loosening her hand from Chris's, she turned and walked rapidly away toward the exit from the Carnival.

"Hey, Toddy, wait up!" Chris called after her. She heard him running behind her. "What's the matter?" he demanded, when he caught up with her.

"I've just had enough, that's all," she replied. "I want to go home now." The hot, choking sensation gripping her throat made it hard to draw a breath.

"Well, sure, Toddy." Puzzled but compliant, Chris fell into step beside her.

They walked back along the quiet, residential streets, the music of the Carnival slowly fading into the distance. At the Hales' gate, they halted.

"Was it anything I said, Toddy?" Chris asked worriedly.

Toddy shook her head. "No, I'm just tired, I guess."

"You *did* have a good time though, didn't you?"

"Oh, yes, Chris. Thanks for taking me,"

she replied quickly.

"And Toddy, you will think about what I asked you, won't you — about my pin?"

"Yes, sure, Chris. But I better go in now."

Chris leaned forward. "May I kiss you good night?"

Toddy hesitated. Then, remembering they had kissed often since Graduation Night, how could she refuse now?

Silently she lifted her face as he bent down to her. Their lips met in a kiss that was sweetly innocent and affectionate.

"I *do* love you, Toddy," Chris said huskily.

"I know," she answered softly, then, "Good night, Chris."

He stood there watching her slim figure in the white dress as she disappeared onto the darkened veranda and through the lighted front door.

On the other side of the door, Toddy stood for a minute trying to compose herself before going up to Helene's room to report on her evening with Chris.

What had come over her at the dancers' booth? It was as though she had suddenly been jerked backward into a half-forgotten world. For a moment she had been terrified. Afraid she would be pulled back into a vortex that would suck her into its depths.

It had been only the blink of an eye actually, but in that brief span of time, she had felt something strong and primal that left her shaken. For that split second she had the illusion that the carnival was more real than her life with the Hales. Did memory have its own truth?

An involuntary shudder swept over her. Toddy shook her head as if to clear it. Then she heard Mrs. Hale's voice.

"Is that you, Toddy? Helene's waiting up for you. Go up and see her so that she can get settled for the night, that's a good girl."

"Yes ma'am, I'm going," Toddy replied. She walked slowly over to the stairway, and stood a moment longer, her hand grasping the newel post. Then straightening her shoulders, she went upstairs.

17

"What are you reading?" Toddy asked Helene as she curled up at the end of her bed.

Helene held up the book.

"It's about Florence Nightingale, the heroine of the Crimean War. She revolutionized nursing and saved hundreds of wounded soldiers' lives by applying the things she had learned at a German nursing school — simple things like cleanliness, things no one seemed to have thought of before," Helene told her. "And she heard God speaking to her, Toddy, telling her what to do."

Toddy sat up straighter, at once intrigued.

"You mean she *actually* heard God's voice? What did it sound like?"

"Well, not as you and I are talking now, but in a very clear way, an inner *knowing*. She was directed to do things, things no one had ever done to take care of the wounded, the sick and dying," Helene explained. "She was truly inspired, she believed, and so was able to be strong and courageous. Would you like to read it? I'm sleepy now so you can take it with you, if you like."

An hour later Toddy was still reading, enthralled by the story of the "Lady With the Lamp." Florence Nightingale was given that name by the soldiers who welcomed the sight of her shadow as she made the rounds at night, moving among their cots, holding her lamp aloft to bring comfort and healing.

Finally, unable to keep her eyes open any longer, Toddy yawned, slid down into the pillows and reluctantly closed the book. She blew out her lamp, but she did not go to sleep right away.

How wonderful to be able to really help the sick and suffering, Toddy thought. And most wonderful of all to know that God had called you to do just that.

Florence Nightingale had started schools in England to train young women to become nurses, Toddy had read. Now there were schools in the United States patterned on her ideas. What a worthwhile way to spend one's life.

She wondered if Miss Tuttle, her old enemy and adversary, had trained in such a school. But Miss Tuttle was no longer around to ask. She had retired a few years ago, gone to live with a sister in Seattle, and had never been replaced. Actually Helene was so much better these days that she did not really need a nurse in attendance.

What if I became a nurse? Toddy thought as she drifted off. Would it be possible? Then if Helene should ever need one, I would be here to take care of her. Maybe she would ask Mrs. Hale, Toddy decided. But first, she would pray about it. Maybe God would tell her what to do, just as He had Florence Nightingale.

The first evening of the Revival Toddy arrived at church with Laurel, and when Kit came in with Miss Cady, all of them sat together in the same pew. So impressed were they by the persuasive preaching of the dynamic Brother Roger Holmes that all three friends were in attendance every night thereafter.

On Friday night the tall, lanky evangelist, attired in a shabby coat and flowing tie, took his place in the pulpit. After the opening prayer, he lifted his great, shaggy head from its bowed position and holding up a few sheets of paper, dramatically tore them into pieces.

"Friends, tonight I am throwing away my prepared sermon notes. I feel led of the Holy Spirit to speak from my heart and from the guidance I feel I've been given." He clasped his hands and bowed his head again for a few minutes. The church was so still that no one seemed to be breathing.

When he raised his head again, he leafed through his worn Bible for another minute before beginning to speak.

"I feel directed to take my text tonight from the Old Testament, Exodus 4, Verse 2: 'What is that in thine hand?' — the question the Lord asked Moses." He allowed his words to hang in the quiet for a moment before continuing, "And Moses looked down at what he perceived as a mere shepherd's stick and replied, 'A rod.'

"To Moses it was a simple, ordinary, everyday object, of little value and certainly of no earthly power. It was not a sword or a lance or a weapon with which Moses could force Pharaoh to release the Hebrew people from their bondage in Egypt. Furthermore, Moses considered himself inadequate for the job — the heroic task of delivering the Jews from captivity. But with God's almighty power, that rod became the miraculous instrument parting the Red Sea so they could escape. Subsequently, it also sent the waters rushing down upon the Egyptian Army in hot pursuit." Brother Holmes paused, his eyes roving over the congregation searchingly.

"Isn't that what we do also? Look at what

we have in our hands, and whine and complain and wonder what we can do with it?" Another pause. "Friends, *whatever* your particular rod, God expects you to *use* it. So I want you to look tonight at *your* rod, at the enormous possibilities within the gifts God has given *you*.

"We each possess very precious gifts which may seem small or commonplace to us, but dedicated to God's will, they can change our lives and the lives of those around us for the better, if we will only take the time to recognize them, dedicate them to God's use."

Brother Holmes leaned forward over the pulpit.

"Power often lies hidden in the obvious," he continued earnestly. "Let us prayerfully look at what lies in our hands and pray to God to show us what He wants us to do with it."

After he finished, there was a hush. His sermon seemed to have had a profound effect on his listeners. No one moved or stirred until Miss Palmtry bustled up to the organ and struck the first few chords of the closing hymn, "Lead Kindly Light."

Slowly the congregation began to file out of the pews, flow into the aisles, and make their way out of the church. There was an absence of the usual greetings and cordial chatter as the people dispersed quietly into the night.

A group of young men, who had remained seated in the back of the church and were the first to leave when the dismissal was given, stood just outside the church steps. Chris detached himself from the group as the girls came out and made his way over to Toddy.

"Can I walk you home?"

"Not tonight, Chris. Kit and I are spending the night at Laurel's."

Disappointed, Chris said, "Oh, well, all right. See you tomorrow then."

The three girls linked arms and started out of the churchyard as the strains of the last hymn floating on the summer air merged with the soft chirpings of crickets outside and the low whinnying of the row of horses tied to the fence around the church.

As if by some unspoken signal, all three began singing the words of the beloved old songs as they walked:

All praise to Thee, my God, This night,
For all the blessings of the light!
Keep me, O keep me, King of kings,
Beneath thine own almighty wings.
O may my soul on Thee repose,
And with sweet sleep mine eyelids close;

Sleep that may me more vigorous make
To serve my God when I awake.

Come unto Me, when shadows darkly
  gather!
When the sad heart is weary and dis-
  tressed,
Seeking for comfort from your heavenly
  Father,
Come unto me and I will give you rest.

The evening air was fresh, cool, delicately
scented with fragrance from all the summer
gardens they passed. Coming through the
Woodwards' gate and entering the shadowy
garden, the three felt a new closeness,
bonded by a shared faith, an unspoken peti-
tion: *What, O Lord, is my "rod" and what do
You wish me to do with it?*

18

"I'm ready to leave now, Mrs. Hale."

Olivia looked up from the evening paper and saw Toddy standing in the doorway of the parlor.

"Oh, yes, the Blanchard dinner party, isn't it?"

"Yes, ma'am," she replied. "New Year's Eve."

"So it is. Well, I suppose it will be a fine affair."

Toddy stood there a moment longer as if waiting for something. She touched her hair tentatively. "Do I look all right?"

Olivia knew the girl was begging for reassurance. Actually, with her golden-red hair swept up, Toddy looked astonishingly grown-up and pretty. The amusing little pixie had become a real beauty. No wonder the Blanchard boy was smitten with her. Toddy kept gazing at her anxiously, waiting. But Olivia did not believe in lavish compliments; they made a person vain.

So, all she did was nod. "Yes, indeed, you look very nice, Toddy."

Toddy smiled and her eyes danced.

Lifting her skirt gracefully, she made a slow pirouette. The velvet bodice of the gown was royal blue; the shirred puffed sleeves and skirt consisted of a pale blue taffeta elaborately flocked in darker blue velvet.

"Thank you! And thank you for this beautiful dress. I do want to look special tonight because all Chris's relatives will be there. I'm a *little* terrified!" she confessed.

A smile tugged at Olivia's mouth. Only Toddy would attempt to describe her feelings so paradoxically.

"How was Helene feeling when you came down?" Olivia asked.

Momentarily Toddy's smile faded. "She *said* she was better. She was resting and thought she would go to sleep soon —" Toddy paused, then asked anxiously, "Do you think I should stay? Not go tonight?"

"No, of course not, child. Helene would be upset if she thought you were missing a party on her account! Mrs. Hubbard is here and surely the two of us can keep an eye on things. I'll go up in a while and see if Helene wants me to read to her until she falls asleep."

Just then the sound of the front doorbell being twisted vigorously echoed through the downstairs. Toddy twirled around and peeked into the hall.

"There's Chris now, come to pick me up!" she exclaimed, starting out of the room.

Impulsively Olivia called to her. "Toddy, just a minute. Come here, please."

Immediately Toddy turned and walked over to stand by Mrs. Hale's chair.

"Yes?"

Lowering her voice, Olivia said, "Don't let Bernice Blanchard intimidate you. She'll try, you know. Just remember, you know which fork to use, and you're charming and considerate. So just be yourself."

Toddy's eyes widened curiously. Mrs. Hale had never said anything like that to her before. She was about to respond when Clara Hubbard appeared in the doorway with Chris, splendid in his evening clothes.

Toddy turned and met Chris's admiring glance.

"Evening, Mrs. Hale," he said politely, but his eyes were on Toddy.

"Good evening, Chris. Have you enjoyed your holidays?"

"Yes, thank you, ma'am." Chris flushed. He was always uncomfortable around the formidable Olivia Hale.

"And how are your studies coming along?"

"Fine thank you, ma'am, that is, except for Trig— Trigonometry and —" he halted, flustered, his face reddening.

"I suppose you've been busy with sports?" Mrs. Hale suggested.

"Well, yes, ma'am, as a matter of fact —"

"And when do you have to return to the University?"

Chris looked gloomy. "Day after to-morrow, I'm afraid."

And none too soon, thought Olivia, not missing Toddy's adoring gaze on him.

Chris shifted uneasily, glanced at Toddy, then said hesitantly, "I guess we better be going. Mother said dinner is going to be served promptly at seven."

"Yes, indeed, you'd best be off then."

"Well, good night, Mrs. Hale," Chris said, obviously eager to go, adding as an afterthought, "And a very Happy New Year."

Olivia smiled wryly. "Thank you, Chris. The same to you."

Watching them leave — the tall, dark-haired boy and the petite, radiant girl — she frowned. Ever since Chris had arrived home for his Christmas vacation, the two of them had spent nearly every day and practically every evening together — ice-skating, sledding, even gift shopping!

She hoped they hadn't any foolish ideas. They were both too young. She dismissed the immediate reminder that she herself had eloped at sixteen with a rough-hewn young man of whom her parents disapproved. In fact, they had never forgiven her for doing so.

Compressing her mouth in a straight line, Olivia's brow furrowed. If they had only been able to leave for Europe in September as she had planned. She had hoped to be away from Meadowridge when Chris came home for the holidays. Their passports had arrived, the girls' wardrobes were assembled and the tickets purchased. Then Helene had had a bad spell and Dr. Woodward had advised against traveling. The summer had been unusually hot, and the heat had apparently taken its toll on her delicate heart.

Their departure was delayed indefinitely. Then, since Olivia was cautioned about an Atlantic crossing in winter, she had postponed their leaving until spring. That is how they happened to still be in Meadowridge when young Blanchard came home from college.

Olivia thought of the day he arrived. One might have thought he had rushed to the house straight from the railroad station, the way he had come bounding up the steps, scarf flying, coattails flapping!

Olivia gave the newspaper a sharp snap. Well, he'd be gone in a few days and things should settle back to normal without Toddy flitting about like a nervous butterfly, dashing in and out, skates dangling over her shoulder, searching for misplaced mittens, rosy-cheeked and starry-eyed. Olivia sighed, as much in regret that her granddaughter could not share such youthful pleasures as in fear of the potential danger of losing Toddy to love.

Toddy and Chris walked from the Hales' house up the hill, their boots crunching in the packed snow, their breath sending frosty plumes into the dark as they talked. They could see the Blanchards' house in the distance, every window alight, sending out rectangles of color onto the crusted snow.

Just as they started up the steps to the veranda encircling the lower story, Chris pulled Toddy gently back toward him. Tilting her chin with one hand, he put the other into his coat pocket and pulled out a spray of mistletoe.

"See? I'm always prepared," he said mischievously, holding it over her head. "An early Happy New Year, Toddy!" He leaned down and touched her lips with his. His kiss was warm and sweet in the cold.

"Happy New Year, Chris," she whispered.

He hugged her, pulling her hard against

him. "I hate to think of leaving you —"

Toddy felt her heart pound. His vacation had been so special. They had hardly had a disagreement, an argument. It had been such a wonderful Christmas. But now it was almost over.

"I'll miss you, too."

"I've a good mind to tell Ma and my father that I'm not going back to the University —" Chris began. "If my father weren't so keen on it —"

"Oh, Chris, you must go back!" Toddy cried in alarm. She drew back and looked up at him. "If you don't, they'll blame *me!*"

At that moment the front door opened and a beam of light enveloped them, and they saw Mrs. Blanchard standing in the doorway.

"Well, for heaven's sake, there you are!" she exclaimed. "We were wondering what was keeping you." She shivered exaggeratedly. "Come in! It's freezing out there. I was just going to send Hugh out to sprinkle some more sand on the path and steps so people wouldn't slip. Hurry, don't let all that cold air into the house, Chris!" She sounded annoyed.

Chris squeezed Toddy's hand in apology and they hurried up the steps and into the house.

Entering the spacious hall, Toddy saw that the whole house was still festively decorated for the holidays. Boughs of evergreens looped with shiny red ribbon adorned the staircase, and the air was spicy with the scent of pine.

Chris helped Toddy off with her coat, then told her to sit down while he knelt to unfasten the gaiters she wore to protect her blue satin slippers. She unwound the crocheted "fascinator" from her head, then craned her neck to admire the beautifully trimmed tree, an eight-foot tall cedar at the foot of the stairs. Gilt garlands glittered in the light from dozens of tiny candles. Glistening balls reflected their sparkle, while brightly painted tin birds nested in the sweeping branches.

"I'll go put these in the cloak room and be right back," Chris told her and disappeared, leaving her alone with Mrs. Blanchard.

Toddy felt the nervous tightening in her stomach. It always happened when she met Chris's mother. Trying to overcome it, she said, "Everything looks lovely, Mrs. Blanchard," she remarked politely.

"Thank you, Toddy. Everyone says I *do* have a certain talent for making things look attractive." Mrs. Blanchard forced a smile which Toddy tried to return with a spontaneous one of her own, but her lips felt stiff.

A small pause then Mrs. Blanchard said, "I'm really surprised you came tonight, Toddy. I heard Helene was far from well." Unmistakably an implied criticism. A definite insinuation that Toddy's place was at Helene's bedside.

"Oh, she's feeling much better, Mrs. Blanchard. Mrs. Hale thinks she overdid at Christmas. Helene adores the holidays and buying gifts and planning surprises for everyone. She loves it all and —"

"You should be very grateful to be in such a lenient household," Mrs. Blanchard cut in coldly. "Sad to say, not all *you orphans* were so fortunate, like that poor — what's her name? — the girl who made the speech at Graduation —"

"Kit Ternan," Toddy supplied between clenched teeth, her fingernails biting into her fisted hands. *Surely* Mrs. Blanchard *must* remember Kit — the first female valedictorian Meadowridge High School ever had!

"Yes, that poor thing in that awful dress! Imagine living out at the Hansens' all these years. *You* could have landed there or in some equally terrible place. You should thank your lucky stars, Toddy."

"Why should Toddy thank her lucky

stars, Ma?" Chris was back, all smiles and glowing happiness.

Mrs. Blanchard looked embarrassed and passed off his question with a shrill little laugh. "Oh, nothing, son. Just girl talk. Now why don't you take Toddy into the parlor and introduce her to your aunts and uncles and cousins? Then have some punch."

"Good idea," Chris agreed heartily and held out his hand to Toddy who took it gratefully. "Come on, Toddy."

Mrs. Blanchard smiled benignly at her son and although Toddy was included, its warmth seemed to evaporate by the time it reached her. Inwardly, Toddy was seething. Chris's mother was either unspeakably rude or completely insensitive. Toddy was included to think it was intended, because she never lost an opportunity to remind Toddy she was an orphan. It was obvious that Mrs. Blanchard was making a very decided point, that Toddy was set apart from the rest of Meadowridge, unacceptable, an outsider forever. How she must hate the idea of Chris being involved with "an Orphan Train rider."

"Did I tell you how smashing you look tonight, Toddy?" Chris whispered as they stood on the threshold of the parlor. Toddy looked up at him with a rush of gratitude.

Who cared what anyone else thought of her, when someone as good-looking and nice as Chris thought she hung the moon?

Dutifully Chris took her around the room, introducing her. The middle-aged uncles were all red-cheeked, balding and jovial, and greeted Toddy with pleasant heartiness. Uncle Jim teased that he did not realize Chris had such good taste, Uncle Cliff gave a friendly wink, while Uncle Murray merely slapped him on the back and grinned.

The aunties were a different cup of tea altogether. They looked remarkably like their sister Bernice. All were plump, with elaborately coiffed hair, wearing a quantity of jewelry and with speculative eyes. Toddy could tell right away that Chris was a favorite nephew and they were sizing her up as to whether she was the right girl for him.

Toddy was appropriately respectful and polite but genuinely relieved when the introductions were over and Chris steered her into the adjoining "second parlor" that had temporarily been turned into a convivial center for the younger members of the clan.

Here she was welcomed as a delightful addition to the gathering. The male cousins clustered around her immediately. Chris's cousin Tom lost no time trying to monopolize her while Roger and Hart circled, waiting for their chance to impress. The four little girl cousins were adorable, much younger than the others, and were happy to watch the "goings on" while each took a turn viewing the stereopticon until dinner was announced.

Toddy was always at her best with people her own age, where her wit and vivacity were a plus. Chris, proud of the good impression she had made on his cousins, manifested not an iota of jealousy.

The dining room looked like a holiday picture. On the embroidered white linen and lace cloth stood two silver candelabra with tall red tapers; in the middle, a centerpiece composed of white carnations ringed in holly, bright with red berries on a footed silver compote. At each place was a small, red-ribboned favor. The red china, edged in gold, was flanked with a formidable array of silver flatware, reminding Toddy of Mrs. Hale's ironic remark: "You know which fork to use —"

As Chris held out her chair, Toddy mentally gritted her teeth, determined to do her upbringing proud.

She took her seat, unfolded her napkin, and looked on either side of her, then down the table to where Mrs. Blanchard simpered, basking in the effusive compliments of her sisters. "Don't let Bernice Blanchard intimidate you. She'll try," Mrs. Hale had said.

Don't worry, I won't, I promise you, Toddy resolved. A small spark of independence flared into flame. She was sorry Chris's mother did not like her, did not approve of her, but she refused to let it spoil her evening. On one side of her was Chris's gallant cousin Hart, and on the other side, his charming little cousin Amelia. Chris himself was smiling at her from across the table.

Annie, the Blanchards' regular maid, almost unrecognizable in a fancy new uniform, was serving the lavish meal with the help of a hired girl. Course followed delicious course — clear soup, salad, white fish, roast lamb, five vegetables, pudding, pecan pie, glazed fruit, marzipan and mints. Mrs. Blanchard had certainly outdone herself in this holiday menu.

But even under her watchful eye, Toddy did not make a single faux pas. Working from the outside in, she even made use of the ivory-handled fruit knife and finger bowls with casual grace.

Knowing she had done well, Toddy was pleased and a little proud of herself — something she was to remember later in the evening. It was in this happy frame of mind, filled with delicious food, flattered by all the attention she had received, that Toddy enthusiastically agreed when the children begged her to join them in a game of hide-and-seek.

After the meal, the gentlemen remained at the table for their brandy and cigars, and the ladies moved to the parlor to chat. So the young folk had the rest of the house in which to play. They counted out who was "It" and then scattered, everyone looking for a good place to hide.

As Toddy stood uncertainly, not knowing which way to go, Chris pointed to the huge blue china vase holding peacock feathers that stood in the hallway outside the parlor door. He was taking the steps two at a time to the landing where a large teakwood Japanese screen would make a great hiding place.

Taking her cue from him, Toddy hurried over and slid behind the vase and, gathering her skirt about her, wedged herself against the wall. Gradually the sounds of running feet and muffled giggles subsided and she guessed everyone had safely hidden themselves. As she crouched there, fragments of the ladies' conversation floated out from the half-closed parlor door.

217

"I thought his being away would lessen the attachment," a voice complained.

"Well, it's been *my* experience that opposition only increases the attraction," said another.

"I definitely agree," someone declared. "You know the old saying, 'Forbidden fruit tastes sweetest!' "

"She's got quite a few airs for someone with no background!"

"But she's a pretty little thing for all that."

"That may well be, Ethel, but surely you can understand how I feel?" That was Mrs. Blanchard speaking.

Suddenly Toddy realized *she* was the topic under discussion. Chris's mother and his aunts were talking about *her!* She felt her face burn while the rest of her turned icy with resentment. Her ears tingled and she put both hands over them, unwilling to hear any more. Shifting her position, ready to move and find another hiding place, she saw Roger who was "It" move across the hall. If he spotted her and called out, the ladies would surely know she had eavesdropped on their conversation.

So she stayed put until Roger passed, heading in the opposite direction. Then very quietly she slipped out from behind the vase and crept up the stairs to join Chris behind the Japanese screen.

He grabbed her hand. "Hey, this is cozy!"

"I have to go home," she said crossly, tugging her hand away.

"Home? Right *now?*" He was surprised. "Why? Aren't you having a good time? We don't have to play with the kids all evening, you know."

Toddy shook her head. "No, I mean, yes. It's not the game, Chris. And I like your cousins. It's just that —" she hesitated unable to think of an excuse. Then she improvised. "I'd like to get home in time to tell Helene good night; she hasn't been feeling well and —"

Chris gave a heavy sigh. "Helene! It's always Helene, Toddy."

"Well, she's my sister and —" Toddy stopped cold. *Was she?* Did Helene *really* consider her a sister? Or was Toddy just *hoping* that she did? The full weight of the things Mrs. Blanchard had said to her earlier and what she had overheard was beginning to reach into that sensitive, vulnerable part of her. All her old insecurity surfaced and unconsciously she shuddered. Tears rushed into her eyes and she turned away quickly so Chris couldn't see them. But he knew he had said something wrong. He touched her arm.

"I'm sorry, Toddy," he said gently. "I didn't mean to offend you. I just — look, if you want to go home, we'll go, right now! As soon as Roger finds us — all right? Don't be mad."

Toddy forced a smile and whispered back, "I'm not mad. Honest. It's just that Helene never gets to go to parties or out very much, and she loves to hear all about everything I do. If she's still awake when I get back — Don't you see, I can share everything that happened with her?"

Well, not *everything,* Toddy amended mentally.

"Sure, Toddy, I understand." He leaned toward her and kissed her lightly, "Did I tell you I think you're the sweetest, most generous —"

Toddy rolled her eyes. "Oh, come on, Chris!"

It was hard for Toddy to face Mrs. Blanchard, tell her she had enjoyed the lovely evening as she said good night. Mrs. Blanchard smiled automatically, but her eyes were as cold as the night outside.

She gazed dotingly on Chris and wagged her finger. "Now Chris, hurry back after you take Toddy home. Uncle Jim wants to have a man-to-man talk with you about college, and they're leaving early in the morning, remember." Then she eyed Toddy with clear intent. "You won't keep him, will you, Toddy? And do wish Mrs. Hale a Happy New Year for me, won't you?"

As they went down the steps and out the gate, Chris took one of Toddy's hands and put it with his into the deep pocket of his coat. The touch of his palm against hers was comforting, but Toddy's heart still stung painfully from the cruel words she had overheard.

"What a night," Chris said, looking up at the sky, a vast dark canopy sprinkled with hundreds of sparkling stars. He squeezed Toddy's hand. "I'm glad you wanted to leave early. We'll get to say Happy New Year to each other alone."

Toddy didn't answer. Her throat was sore with distress. The cutting conversation had hurt. Like a hangnail or a stone bruise, it was there, no matter how she tried to dismiss it.

To Mrs. Blanchard, she would always be one of those "Orphan Train" waifs — unsuitable, unacceptable, unworthy of her son. Nothing Toddy could say or do or become would change that. Loving Chris, his loving her, made no difference. They would never overcome his mother's objections.

"Toddy —" Chris stopped under a lamp-post and put his hands on her shoulders, slowly turning her around to the light so he could see her face. "Ma was right about Uncle Jim's wanting to talk to me," he began, his voice intense as he went on, "But it isn't about college. I already broached the subject to *him* earlier, but we haven't had a chance to be alone yet. Too many people, too many relatives around." Chris went on with mounting excitement. "What I *really* wanted to talk to Uncle Jim about was . . . going to work for him. You see, he has a construction firm in Brookhaven, a town about fifty miles from here. You know I've always liked working with my hands and being out of doors! I hate the thought of working in a bank, like my father. Ma only likes the idea because it's a kind of prestigious job." He hesitated. "So, what do you think? If he'd let me go to work for him, I'd quit college after this semester, and then — and then, Toddy, I could support a wife — I mean, Toddy, you *know* how much I love you — there's never been anyone else but you. Would you marry me?"

Stunned, Toddy stared back at Chris. "But, Chris, your parents would never agree to that!"

His handsome face grew stubborn.

"I don't want to go back to the University. I don't want to wait three more years." His hands gripped her shoulders tightly. "I'm afraid something will happen. I'm afraid I'll lose you."

A dozen conflicting thoughts rushed into Toddy's mind. There was no doubt of the love she saw in Chris's eyes, heard in his voice, felt in his touch, his kiss. The three months he had been gone she had missed him more than she thought possible. These two weeks he'd been home for the holidays had been heaven.

For a moment a wonderful fantasy unfolded, a fairy tale come true. She and Chris, childhood friends, high-school sweethearts, meant for each other, destined for happiness. What else did they need but each other?

A home of her own, something Toddy had always longed for, someone to love her, someone she could love and cherish and care for, and like her favorite storybook endings, live with "happily ever after." Could that really happen for her and Chris? He was saying it could, was telling her it was possible.

"Well, what do you say, Toddy? Will you? You *do* love me, don't you?"

Toddy shivered suddenly.

Quickly Chris put his arm around her, drew her close so that her cheek was against the rough tweed of his coat.

"You don't need to answer that. I know you do. And we'll work it out. Come on, you're getting cold. I'll get you home. Then, tonight, I'll talk to Uncle Jim. I'll get him to talk to my folks, convince them that it's what I want to do —"

The temperature had dropped and now the sidewalks were crusted over with a thin layer of ice. Chris's arm was around Toddy as they hurried along. The air was so cold it was almost hard to draw a deep breath. As they rounded the corner and started up the hill toward the Hales' house, Toddy stopped short. She clutched Chris's arm.

"Oh, Chris, look!" she gasped. "That's Dr. Woodward's buggy in front of the house! Helene must be worse! O dear Lord!" And Toddy broke away from Chris and started to run.

Toddy huddled on the top step of the stairway, a few feet from Helene's bedroom door. Shivering, she crossed her arms, hugging herself as she rocked back and forth.

"Oh, please dear God, help Helene, help her get well!" Toddy prayed desperately.

Ever since she had rushed into the house a

few hours ago and had seen Clara Hubbard's red-rimmed eyes, Toddy had been locked in misery. In a few words, Clara told her what had happened. Sometime in the middle of the evening Helene had begun to have trouble breathing. Gradually the spell grew worse and Mrs. Hale summoned Dr. Woodward. Shortly after he arrived, Helene had had a heart seizure.

"Thank God, the doctor was here!" mumbled Clara, sniffling, holding a crumpled handkerchief to her mouth.

All the blood in Toddy's body seemed to turn to ice water. Her teeth began to chatter and she had to clench them to stop. Deep shuddering waves of panic threatened to engulf her. Only by sheer willpower was she able to prevent breaking into sobs. Helene had had "spells" before, but nothing like this. Hovering outside the closed door, Toddy had heard her rasping gasps for breath. Toddy bit her lip, fighting back the choking sobs. "Please, God, please!" she begged, the rest of her prayers wordless.

She knew it was not right to bargain with God, but that night as she cried out to Him, Toddy's plea repeated itself endlessly. "If You'll just let Helene get well, I'll be so good. I'll not pose in front of the mirror, or try to be witty or make fun of

Miss Tuttle or imitate people! I'll not show off or anything, Lord. Please! I'll devote my whole life to Helene, if You'll just make her well now."

Unorthodox as her prayers were, they were straight from her aching heart. Helene was her *sister,* no matter what anyone else said! Of all the people in her life, Toddy knew Helene was the only one who loved her just as she was! If she lost Helene, how empty the world would be.

From out of the past came the jeering voice of Paula, the housemaid, long gone to wherever departing housemaids go. Still, her spiteful words echoed clear and loud in Toddy's memory. "If anything happens to Miss Helene, mark my words, you'd be out on your ear, quick as a wink!" Toddy had pretended not to care, but the warning had left deep scars in her soul.

Remembering them now, Toddy felt herself shrink back into that former state of insecurity. What *would* happen to *her* if Helene — Toddy hugged her arms about herself. She wouldn't even think about it. Nothing was going to happen to Helene. Please, God!

Just then Helene's door opened and Dr. Woodward stepped out into the hall, followed by Mrs. Hale. Toddy scrambled up from where she sat, stepped back into the shadows.

"Well, she's passed this crisis," Dr. Woodward said. "She'll probably sleep for a few hours. But she's not to be left alone. Someone should be at her bedside in case her breathing becomes labored again —"

"Was this — *serious?*" Mrs. Hale asked. "I mean, more than a complication of the cold she caught coming home from the Christmas church service?"

"In Helene's state of health, *anything* can be serious," Dr. Woodward replied.

"I wish we could have gotten away sooner!" fretted Mrs. Hale. "I had hoped to spend the winter in Italy, hoped the warm Mediterranean climate would —" she halted. "You know I was planning to take the girls to Europe in March, Dr. Woodward. Should I wait until spring?"

There was a long pause, and Toddy held her breath.

Then Dr. Woodward sighed. "My dear Mrs. Hale, I don't think *when* you go makes a great deal of difference."

"Do you mean — do you think the trip would be too much for Helene?"

"What I'm trying to say in the kindest way, Mrs. Hale, is that it doesn't matter whether she goes to Europe or stays in

Meadowridge. Helene is only twenty-three, but she has the heart of a person three times her age, and it is wearing out. I have to tell you Helene may have only a year or less to live."

Toddy was not sure whether it was Mrs. Hale's moan or her own she heard. She brought her hands to her mouth, the knuckles pressing hard against her lips.

A year! One year, twelve months. Helene had only a year to live! Dr. Woodward's pronouncement repeated itself endlessly in Toddy's brain.

Gone were all those fantasies of running away with Chris, of the two of them living in a little cottage somewhere together, running hand-in-hand forever through fields of daisies. It was a dream. A childish dream to be put away with all other childish things.

If Helene only had a year, Toddy would devote herself totally to making it the best, the happiest year she had ever known. Whatever it took, whatever she had to give up, that's what she would do!

19

Germany
Winter 1902

In the mirrored elegance of the dining room at the German hotel, Olivia Hale sipped her after-dinner coffee, her expression thoughtful as she observed the two girls sitting opposite her at the table. Toddy and Helene were at one of their favorite games — the theme being to imagine the life stories of their fellow diners, providing them with fantasy backgrounds, purposes and destinies. Most of the time they played it with sly subtlety and yet it was usually accompanied by suppressed giggles and, occasionally, unrepressed hilarity. Since most of the other guests at the luxurious hotel neither spoke nor understood English, the game was fairly free from detection by their "victims."

Olivia was glad the two girls could find some relief in this innocent pastime since otherwise their sojourn in Munich would have been completely without pleasure for Helene and probably tediously boring for Toddy. They were here for Helene to be examined by a famous German specialist at the recommendation of her Swiss doctor.

Ironically, his diagnosis had supported that of Dr. Lee Woodward in Meadowridge. So all Olivia's desperate search for a cure or more optimistic prognosis for Helene's condition had been futile. All the traveling, the consultations, the clinics and the enthusiastic endorsements for this treatment or that had all, in the end, proven fruitless.

Unconsciously Olivia sighed, observing her two companions. While Toddy's complexion glowed and her hair had a healthy sheen as a result of their weeks in Switzerland, Helene, by comparison, looked frailer, paler, her dark eyes larger in her thin face.

Olivia felt a stab of resentment. Why? Why *Helene?* What good was all her money, enabling her to take her granddaughter anywhere on the globe, seek the finest doctors known, if it could not bring health and well-being to this dear girl?

Suddenly Olivia felt weary. She was tired of traveling, tired of foreign countries, alien ways, people speaking languages she could not understand. She was tired of consulting her phrase book in order to accomplish the most ordinary task. She longed for the simplicity of life back in Meadowridge. She wanted to be in her own comfortable house, eating food without strange names. She wanted to sleep in her own bed. Olivia wanted to go home.

Just then there was a burst of lighthearted laughter from across the table and Helene buried her mouth in her napkin while Toddy reached for a glass of water as though choking.

Irrepressible youth! No matter what she had been through as far as examinations, unpalatable medicine, exhausting treatments, Helene had maintained her zest for life, her sense of humor, her sweet disposition. And, of course, Toddy was the source of much of it.

At this moment, their waiter approached, his erect bearing that of a Prussian officer. With a stiff bow, he asked in almost unintelligible guttural English: "Vill der be anysing else, Modam?"

"I think not," Olivia replied and signed the check he presented on a small silver tray. Rising from her chair, she asked, "Ready, girls?"

Toddy and Helene exchanged a glance.

"We thought we might wait in the salon for a while, Grandmother, to listen to the music and watch the dancing," Helene replied, her eyes twinkling.

Olivia's mouth twisted in a smile. She

knew it was an excuse to continue their naughty game. She had heard them laughingly discuss the stiff formal atmosphere of the hotel, its middle-aged, overweight guests, all of whom behaved like royalty. She knew they found the social scene in the stodgy hotel ludicrous.

Well, she couldn't blame them if they found it a source of amusement. There certainly had not been much in the way of entertainment for young people during their stay here. Especially for Toddy, so full of life and energy. Not that she ever complained. She seemed completely devoted to Helene, only wanting to be with her. She even accompanied her to her doctor's appointments, spending hours in waiting rooms. Then afterwards, when Helene was fatigued from her ordeal, Toddy would remain in her room, reading aloud to her until she fell asleep. No real sisters could have been closer. Thank God for Toddy, Olivia thought.

Toddy and Helene soon tired of the game since the dancers were few and completely impassive, oblivious to the music and their partners. They soon followed Olivia up to the suite they had occupied since their arrival in Germany.

"I'll go say good night to Grandmother,

then I'll be in," Helene told Toddy when they got off the elevator.

Toddy was sitting up in bed braiding her hair when Helene came in about a half-hour later.

Helene looked pensive as she sat at the foot of the bed and watched Toddy for a few minutes silently.

"Anything the matter?" Toddy asked.

"I think Grandmother wants to go home, Toddy."

"To Meadowridge? But I thought she meant to go back to France, to Paris."

"She did, at first, but now she says she's anxious to get back to the States, to get settled in her own home again. I think she feels we've been gone long enough." Helene's eyes were troubled. "The *real* reason, I think, is what she's *not* saying, Toddy. She's discouraged, disappointed that the European doctors she was told so much about can't fix my heart!" Helene gave a little shrug. "But then nobody could do that! Dr. Lee warned her before we left not to be too optimistic. I overheard them talking —"

Something cold clutched Toddy's heart. She hoped Helene had not overheard that ominous prediction.

"So, then we'll be leaving to go back . . . soon?"

"That's what we were talking about. I told her I wanted to discuss it with you. Because, you see, Toddy, I have an idea." Helene paused, then leaned over and took Toddy's hand in both her own.

"Toddy, I've always wanted to spend Christmas in Austria. You know there seems something very special about that country to me. It was the place where my favorite Christmas carol, 'Silent Night,' was composed in a little village not far from Salzburg." She took a big breath. "What would you think of letting Grandmother go ahead to London and arrange for our passage home while we — you and I — stay on another few weeks and celebrate Christmas in Austria?"

"What would your grandmother say to that?" Toddy asked cautiously.

"I'm sure she'd be agreeable if you are." Helene smiled. "It's not as though we were children anymore. You're twenty and I'm almost twenty-five and after all it *is* 1902! We're living in the Twentieth Century, not the Dark Ages!"

So it was decided that Mrs. Hale would go to England by herself. There, from the comfort of her suite at the Claridge Hotel, she would make arrangements for the return trip to the States. When the girls joined her there at the first of the year, they would be able to enjoy some theater and shopping and sightseeing in London before their sailing date.

It was with much excitement and an elevated sense of independence that the two boarded the train in Munich for Salzburg and from there to travel to the Alpine valley of Badgastein, a renowned health resort. For centuries it had been a popular resort for vacationing kings, emperors, maharajahs, statesmen, Europeans listed in the Almanach de Gotha, as well as world-famous artists, such as Wagner.

The deciding factor in Mrs. Hale's concession to Helene's request was that she would also be getting the restorative benefits of this notable spa.

But as the two young women got off the train at the station and saw the picturesque Austrian village, they could not have been more delighted at its endless possibilities for a holiday.

Floating through the clear, crystal air was the sound of Viennese music, provided by a band attired in colorful Tyrolean costume. The winding streets were thronged with tourists and townspeople alike, all dressed in traditional costumes — the men in embroidered vests, lederhosen, and ribboned knee socks; the women in tight velvet basques and swinging flowered skirts, accompanied by cherubic, rosy-cheeked children looking like miniature replicas of their parents. The shop windows were bright with all sorts of intriguing gifts, and the streets were gaily decorated for the season.

"It looks exactly like one of those toy villages people set up under their Christmas trees, doesn't it?" exclaimed Helene, squeezing Toddy's arm.

The hotel had sent its horse-drawn sleigh to take them up the snowy hill to the rambling, rustic brown chalet surrounded by green-black evergreens. Perched on a cliff, it commanded a magnificent view of a waterfall and bridge so ethereally beautiful that Toddy was reminded of an Impressionistic painting.

The chalet had a fairy-tale look with its carved and fancifully painted eaves, sharply contrasting to the formal German hotel with its stiff, uniformed staff. Inside, there were no marble pillars or potted palms, but a roaring fire blazing in the wide stone fireplace, and comfortable furniture. Everyone was friendly and smiling, the atmosphere warm and welcoming.

A bellhop, fresh-faced as a choirboy, took Toddy and Helene up a broad staircase to their adjoining rooms. Each one opened out onto its own little balcony. The furnishings were simple — a glossy wood floor, white walls, a handsome, hand-painted Austrian armoire, an alcoved bed, covered with a white eiderdown quilt and piles of feather pillows into which one sank luxuriously.

Helene was given her spa schedule which sounded interesting and not stringently therapeutic. In each room there was a map of the hotel grounds, indicating the pathways for walks, punctuated by directions to coffee shops as rewards at the ends of the routes.

"This will be a wonderful vacation!" declared Helene, looking happier than Toddy had seen her in weeks. A dart of hope sprang up in Toddy. Maybe this more relaxed environment was just what Helene needed.

So began a fortnight of serene days filled with interesting new experiences and happy events. Helene's mornings were taken up with her prescribed treatment, followed by an hour's rest. Then Toddy met her for lunch — sometimes in the hotel's outdoor restaurant, where, incredibly warm and comfortable, they sat in bright sunshine while surrounded by snow-covered hills glistening like gems. Afternoons they spent strolling the various walks and exploring the fascinating shops in town, ending up in one of the coffee shops to sip café mocha, topped with swirls of whipped cream, and to listen to Viennese waltzes from the band-stand in the center of town.

"It's all so magical!" Toddy sighed ecstatically.

"It's a long way from Meadowridge, isn't it?" laughed Helene.

At that moment Toddy noticed a passing group of young men in lederhosen and jaunty Tyrolean hats. Strangely, something about one of them reminded her of Chris Blanchard. For one brief moment Toddy felt a sharp twinge of regret. It came and went in an instant. It was all for the best, she told herself. After all, it was she who had broken off their romance, given him his freedom to find someone else. There was no room in her life now for romantic plans.

Later, when Toddy remembered these weeks she and Helene had spent together in Badgastein, it would seem an endless stream of happy days — each one a wonderful gift to be opened and enjoyed.

As Christmas drew near, they became very secretive, going their separate ways on afternoon shopping excursions as each planned surprises for the other. Spending Christmas so far from home took on a very special meaning to both of them.

Two days before Christmas Eve there was a parade through the middle of town with the arrival of "St. Nicholas," the Austrian version of Santa Claus, dressed regally in a red velvet cape trimmed with ermine. The jolly "saint" passed out delicious chocolate candies and exquisite marzipan, an almond-based confection, in the shapes of fruit. People lined the streets to cheer him and shout as he passed by, calling back the greeting, *"Froehliche Weinachten."*

Their arms full of mysterious purchases, the girls hurried back to the hotel on foot in the early darkness amidst white curtains of softly falling snow. Helene squeezed Toddy's arm as they entered the chalet.

"Oh look, Toddy, how beautiful!"

Inside, in the center of the lobby, stood a Christmas tree in sparkling splendor, its shining star nearly touching the vaulted ceiling. Decorated with beautiful orna-ments — angels, birds, flowers, painted balls, draped with gilt garlands, hung with silvery tinsel — the tree gleamed with dozens of tiny candles.

"Oh, isn't it all perfect, Toddy?" sighed Helene happily.

But when they got to their rooms and dumped their packages, Toddy thought

Helene looked pale and drained. Toddy insisted they order room service to bring their supper up so she could get into bed and rest.

When Helene protested, Toddy reminded her, "Remember there's to be a party for the hotel guests tomorrow, and you don't want to be worn out and miss it."

But Helene did miss it. Too weak to get up the next morning, she sent down word to the hotel doctor that she could not come for her usual appointment, and he dropped by later to check her condition. Toddy blamed herself for crowding too much into these days before Christmas, and promised herself that from now on she would make sure to slow down the pace of their activities. Helene, as cheerful as ever, reassured Toddy that *she* had overdone and only needed to rest a bit.

Still feeling too weak to attend the gala party Christmas Eve in the lobby, Helene insisted Toddy go. Reluctantly she complied, but did not stay long and came back upstairs shortly, bringing the gift that had been placed on the tree for Helene, along with eggnog and all sorts of cookies and other goodies so they could have their own Christmas party.

When they heard the church bells ringing, they bundled up and went out on the balcony to watch the procession of towns-people in their traditional folk costumes walking by on their way to attend Midnight Mass. To Helene's joy, they were singing her favorite carol in German, *"Stille Nacht, Heilige Nacht."*

"Oh, Toddy, this *has* to be my happiest Christmas ever —" she sighed.

Awakened on Christmas morning by the maid bringing her breakfast, Toddy was alarmed to find a note from the hotel doctor asking her to come to his office. As soon as she was dressed, after peeking into Helene's room and seeing she was still asleep, Toddy went straight downstairs.

The doctor wasted no words. "Your sister's condition is deteriorating," he told her gravely. "The treatments we have suggested are only a palliative, giving her temporary relief, but we cannot stop the progress of her disease."

Toddy felt a cold tide of fear wash over her.

"Miss Hale is living on borrowed time. Every day is a miracle."

Toddy's hands clenched in her lap. "What do you suggest we do?"

Dr. Ludwig shook his head and stroked his well-trimmed beard thoughtfully for a moment. "I cannot advise travel, it would be dangerous, but you two young ladies are alone and very far from home —" he paused significantly. "I think you should notify Miss Helene's grandmother —"

Toddy left the doctor's office as if in a trance. Instead of returning to her room where Helene would hear her come in and call to her, Toddy went outside and blindly turned onto one of the trails that wound through the snow-drifted woods. Unthinking, she took the one marked the Empress Elizabeth Walk, named after the mother of the tragic Crown Prince Rudolf who had died mysteriously at the Royal Hunting Lodge. It was said that it was along this path the heartbroken mother often walked, mourning her only son.

Toddy's own heart was near breaking. The vague anxiety she had always felt about Helene descended like a leaden weight. All the hopeful signs she had looked for with this change of scene she now realized were mostly her own wishful thinking. The snow-sparkled scenery about her dimmed as tears flooded her eyes.

Helene's time was nearly up, her days numbered. The fear the Hale household had lived with but never spoke of openly, was about to come upon them. Did Helene realize it, too?

Why? Oh, why must Helene be taken away from her? Bitter sobs rushed up into Toddy's throat, and she halted on the path. Leaning her arm against a tree, she put her head upon it and wept.

At length, she straightened up. The tears had not eased the pain, but they had strengthened her spirit.

"If we only have this time, it will be the best of all possible times," Toddy resolved. She wiped her eyes, blew her nose and, turning, walked back to the hotel. Helene was asleep when she looked in on her, so Toddy had a chance to compose herself before Helene awakened. By then, Toddy was her old merry self, regaling Helene with droll imitations of the porter, the desk clerk and any number of characters she had observed or drew from her own fertile imagination. If Toddy had ever doubted her acting ability, she could no longer deny it now.

Hard as she tried to keep up a brave front, when Helene awakened she looked up suddenly and saw Toddy gazing at her with wistful eyes.

Helene reached out and covered Toddy's hand with her own thin one, saying tenderly, "Toddy, dear, don't be sad, please. I know, and it's all right. I've known for a long time. I'm not in any pain physically or too unhappy about the fact that I won't get well."

"But you *must* get well, Helene!" Toddy said fiercely while tears streamed down her cheeks. "We'll go somewhere else, find another doctor. I won't accept it! I'll keep praying and —"

"Don't distress yourself for my sake," Helene said softly. "Let's enjoy what we have. Now, this day, this very minute."

Toddy slipped out of her chair, knelt beside Helene, holding onto her hand, her head against Helene's knee.

"I can't lose you, Helene," she sobbed. "There must be something we can do!"

Helene smoothed Toddy's unruly curls. "Toddy, would it help to know *you* have made all the difference in my life? Dear little sister, without you my life would have been so drab, so lonely —"

In spite of trying to be brave, Helene began to cry also and for a while the two girls clung to each other helplessly, their tears mingling.

They talked for a long time, sharing all the deep things in their hearts, agreeing to make the best of the time they had together. Then, noticing Helene's pallor, Toddy insisted she not talk anymore, just rest.

As it turned out, their time together was shorter than they had guessed.

The next morning Helene was too weak and ill to get up, and Toddy sent for the doctor.

Toddy refused to leave her and that afternoon as she sat by her bedside, Helene slipped quietly away. When the doctor came again, Toddy was still holding her hand.

Numbed by her grief, Toddy walked outside into the fading daylight. Directionless, overwhelmed by the enormity of her loss, she continued through the village, crossed over the little arched bridge at the end of the street, and found herself in the churchyard of a small Baroque chapel. She pushed open the doors and walked inside. Only a flickering lamp near the altar illuminated the interior; there was a quietness within that comforted Toddy as she advanced up the short aisle to the wooden kneelers in front of a small altar.

She lowered herself and knelt, feeling the peace of the place wrap around her like a cloak. All the questions she had had about Helene's being taken from her rose, demanding answers. But all that came into her mind were the remembered Scripture verses: "Be still and know that I am God. . . . My thoughts are not your thoughts, nor are my ways your ways."

Toddy did not know how long she knelt there, but as she got to her feet and started out of the chapel, she saw a wall plaque on which was lettered in the artistic German script: *"Auf Wiedersehen."*

In English she knew that meant "Farewell. Goodbye. Until we meet again."

Softly Toddy whispered, *"Auf Wiedersehen,* dear Helene."

20

It was to a devastated Mrs. Hale Toddy returned when she reached London. Although they had both known for some time that Helene's life hung by a thread, the realization that she was dead was difficult for both of them to absorb.

Mrs. Hale seemed unable to think or act in her normal efficient manner, so it was Toddy who took charge of making their reservations and the arrangements for Helene's body to accompany them on the long, sad journey home.

While they awaited their departure date, the gray drab English winter weather did nothing to lift the sense of depression which weighed so heavily on both of them. They missed Helene as much when they were together as when each was alone. Soon Toddy realized her presence was a poignant reminder to Mrs. Hale of the granddaughter she had lost, and began to keep to herself.

The earliest possible sailing date was three weeks after her arrival in London and in the long days that followed, Toddy had much time to think about the past, ponder the present, and worry about the future.

On the solitary walks she took along the strange city streets and through its parks, under skies gray with fog, Toddy's heart was heavy, her thoughts troubled. Out of the past rushed that old fear, the voices taunting, "If anything happens to Helene —"

Now something *had* happened to Helene. Now that she was gone, what was to become of Toddy?

The bitterness of her first grief had dulled somewhat. Not for anything would Toddy wish Helene back to the wasting pain of her illness. Helene had gone sweetly, quietly, had not suffered at the last. With all her ardent faith Toddy *knew* Helene was at peace, joyful, healed. It was just that nothing or no one could fill that void created by Helene's passing. The whole world seemed empty now that that one dear face was missing.

At length, it was time for them to board their ship. Almost immediately Mrs. Hale retired to her own cabin and kept to it for most of the week's voyage. On this crossing, Toddy was not a part of the group of young people laughing, playing shuffleboard and deck tennis, dancing late into the night in the social lounge. She remained part, except at mealtimes, when she sat at her assigned table and bravely tried to carry on pleasant conversation with the other passengers. The rest of the time she walked the deck, or sat bundled in her deck chair looking out at the sea that brought her, day by day, closer and closer to the time of decision.

She went over and over in her mind what she should do. The open book in her lap lay unread as she stared out into space, trying to see into her own future. Once back in Meadowridge, Mrs. Hale would not need her. She was a strong woman who had already survived other tragedies. Toddy felt she could not expect to remain part of the Hale household now that the reason she had been brought there was gone.

She must do something useful with her life. With dismay, she realized that she had never had long-term goals. Not like Kit, who wanted to write, nor did she have a glorious singing voice like Laurel. She had been in love with Chris and thought they would marry. Then that dream had been put aside when she decided to devote herself to Helene until —

She had sent Chris away, and she did not regret that, although there was still a bruised spot in her heart when she thought of him. She had done the right, the fair thing, and by now Chris probably had found someone else to make him happy. She wasn't going to look back at what might have been.

But now, with Helene gone, Toddy wanted *her* life to count for something.

Two days out of New York, Toddy paced the deck deep in thought. At one point she halted to lean against the rail. Thoughts of Helene were very strong.

Oh, Helene, if you were only here to advise me, to help me, to tell me what I should do. Toddy sighed in despair.

She could imagine Helene whispering, "Pray about it, Toddy, dear," and she felt a certain lifting of her spirit.

Of course, that's what she *should* have been doing all along! But Toddy had found it hard to pray since Helene's death. She would begin and then her thoughts would drift, remembering snatches of conversations, some of the experiences they had shared, the people they had met on their travels. What started out as prayers often became melancholy reminiscences.

But as she stood there, the wind tugging at her hat and veil, Toddy did pray. The words of a Psalm came to mind: "Show me Thy ways, O Lord, teach me Thy paths. Lead me in Thy truth and teach me, For

Thou art the God of my salvation." It was almost as if she had been guided to pray from Scripture, but she added her own postscript, "Lord, You know me. My good points and bad ones, my abilities and my weaknesses. You know my heart. Lead me in the direction You would have me go, give me a purpose in life."

The last night on shipboard before their scheduled docking the next morning, Mrs. Hale called Toddy into her stateroom.

"Toddy, there are some things we need to talk about," she began. "I've been thinking of a memorial service for Helene when we get back to Meadowridge and I want you to choose an inscription for a headstone that would be appropriate for her. You were closer to her than anyone, Toddy, so you would know what she would like best —"

Toddy felt a lump rising in her throat that made it difficult for her to reply. The request made Helen's death heartbreakingly real.

"Yes, I'll think about it," she promised.

"And there's something else, Toddy, I've meant to speak to you about before, but now is as good a time as any. Now that Helene is gone, you must begin to think of your own future. You know how much Helene loved you, Toddy. What you may not know is that she was independently wealthy. She inherited a great deal of money from her father, my son."

She halted again. "I could explain all the legalities, but what matters is that Helene had a long talk with me when you graduated from high school. Helene always knew that her life hung by a fragile thread and insisted on making out a will before we left for Europe. You, Toddy, are her chief beneficiary."

Toddy looked uncomprehendingly at Mrs. Hale.

"Yes, you heard me correctly. She left most of her estate to you," she said as if anticipating Toddy's disbelief. "She wanted you to be free and independent as she was. The difference is that you have the health to travel, to accomplish your goals. I am, of course, the guardian of the trust fund she had set up for you. Until you are twenty-one, my signature will be required on any expenditures or withdrawals you make, my approval necessary for any investment." Mrs. Hale regarded Toddy sharply. "Do you understand what this means?"

Toddy nodded. "I think so."

"If you want to go to college, or return to Europe or pursue a career — We need to talk to Mr. Blanchard at the bank about your funds and how you choose to spend them."

Up until that moment Toddy's decision had not been definite. Suddenly Toddy felt what must be God's will for her life.

Her voice sounded surprisingly strong, even to herself. "I think I *have* decided, Mrs. Hale. I believe I would like to be a nurse, to enter nurses' training."

Mrs. Hale nodded her head slowly, as if considering the idea.

"A splendid idea, Toddy. You'll make a fine nurse. You're intelligent, compassionate, energetic. Your personality is steady and cheerful. Yes, Helene would be pleased."

21

1903–1904

The rising bell shrilled down the hall, echoing into every cubicle of the probationers' dormitory in the Nurses' Training School, Good Samaritan Hospital.

Toddy moaned, pulled the blanket up over her head, burying her face in her pillow. Only a faint gray light seeped in through the high windows on this winter-dark morning. She squeezed her eyes shut more tightly. Could she possibly sneak ten more minutes of sleep?

All around her Toddy heard familiar sounds coming from her awakening fellow student nurses — similar protesting groans, creaking bedsprings, opening drawers, swishing water being poured into wash-bowls.

Five-thirty! Only twenty minutes to get up, put on her pink muslin uniform, button on the starched white pinafore, pull on and garter the black cotton stockings, lace up and tie the sensible black duty shoes. Then wash her face, brush her unruly curls, twist her hair into the severe topknot and secure it with pins, fling the dark blue, red-lined cape around her shoulders and run downstairs and across the quadrangle to the chapel for morning prayers. After that, over to the hospital dining room, bolt a breakfast of oatmeal and coffee, and report to duty on the ward by seven sharp.

Upon signing in and checking for any special assignments in the Head Nurse's duty book, there would not be a minute Toddy could call her own for the next twelve hours. First, sweep and mop the ward floor, scrub every unoccupied bed with disinfectant and change the sheets. Then, while the Third Year students bathed the patients and prepared them for the day, six-month probationers such as Toddy set up breakfast trays. While the patients were eating or being fed, "probies" were sent down to the basement to pick up coal for their ward and carry the loaded scuttles back upstairs for the stove at the end of each corridor. Next the water pitchers for each patient's bedside table must be filled and distributed.

At nine, the staff doctors made rounds, accompanied by the ward nurse and followed by the student nurses who took notes while the charts were checked and any new diagnosis was made or new medication prescribed. The students were well advised to pay close attention since they would later be quizzed on the chart sessions. At ten, they were due in class in the school building. Two hours later, back to the wards for lunch tray distribution.

A half-hour break followed, giving little time to eat their own lunch and review any lessons before afternoon classes which lasted until three. Back on the wards at four where, supervised by the Third-Year students, they gave back rubs, refilled water pitchers, freshened the patients and readied them for Visitors Hours, and worked in the linen room, folding and sorting.

At five, dinner trays were brought up from the kitchen. Again, probies distributed and collected them. Six was their own dinner hour, followed by a half-hour recreation period before they were to report back to their wards to help get patients settled for the night.

At nine, when they returned to the Nurses' Home and their own "cubes," there were still tomorrow's lessons to be studied, papers to write, chart notes to be reviewed. At ten, when the "Lights Out" bell rang, Toddy usually could barely hold her eyes open.

She had never imagined nurses' training

would be so rigorous. Most of her class-mates were hearty farm girls from the Mid-west, used to hard chores at home and not delicate boned like Toddy. But what she lacked in physical strength, Toddy made up in enthusiasm and energy and a fierce deter-mination to succeed in her chosen vocation. She had a real empathy for the patients and most enjoyed caring for them.

The discipline was harsh. It was the pur-pose of the school to weed out early the young women who would not make good nurses. The requirements for graduation, the solemn "capping" ceremony, awarding the symbol of each young woman's success, were stringent. Not only was a thorough knowledge of anatomy, physiology, chem-istry, and pharmacology demanded, but the understanding of the procedure of pre-scribed treatment as well as its application.

There were, however, subtler, other infi-nitely more important aspects of the would-be nurses' personalities that were carefully noted, observed, marked by their teachers, their supervisors, and the doctors they at-tended. Did this person have the necessary skills, the patience, the reassuring pres-ence, the serenity in a crisis to instill in the sick or injured patient the confidence that he was being cared for in the best and most effective manner?

The first weeks she was at Good Samaritan, Toddy was not even sure she would make it through her six-month probationary period. Sometimes, dragging up to her cubicle after a seemingly endless day, she would throw herself across her cot, fatigued, frustrated, filled with the gnawing uncertainty that perhaps she had made a dreadful mistake. Maybe she was not cut out to be a nurse.

In spite of doubts, reinforced by Miss Pryor's often cutting reprimands, Toddy got through her probationary period, and traded her pink uniform for the blue-striped one with its high, stiff collar and white-bibbed apron of the Student Nurse. When particularly discouraged or worn out, she would strengthen her resolve by repeating the reassuring verse from Philippians: "Being confident of this very thing, that he which hath begun a good work in you will complete it." She had come here believing it was God's will for her life, and she would trust Him to see her through.

But if she thought those first months were hard she had a further eye-opening when she entered into the second half of her training.

Everything was more intense and demanding — the studies, the ward work, the constant supervision by relentlessly exacting superiors. Every nine weeks the student nurses were assigned to different wards under different head nurses. Each one, with different expectations and different requirements, took getting used to. While students were expected to make these adjustments, they were at the same time learning new skills, sharpening their observation abilities, noticing and charting changes in patients, and following directions, all the while trying to be cheerful, prompt, and attentive.

One afternoon Toddy was taking a well-deserved break in her dormitory room before going on the second half of her shift, when one of the probies stuck her head in the door and announced she had a visitor in the guest parlor. Puzzled, Toddy got up from where she was curled on her cot, straightened her hair, smoothed her apron and went downstairs.

"Hello, Toddy," a familiar voice greeted her as she came in the parlor door.

Toddy blinked her eyes. To her surprise it was Bernice Blanchard, Chris's mother, sitting primly in one of the parlor chairs.

"Mrs. Blanchard!" she gasped. "How — how nice to see you!"

"Well, Toddy, you look well." Mrs.

Blanchard's eyes took in every inch. "You are probably wondering why I'm here. Well, Mr. Blanchard had to attend a Banking Conference in St. Louis and I decided it was too good an opportunity to miss, so I came with him. I saw your —" she halted a second, then said, "I saw *Mrs. Hale* at church last Sunday and she told me you were at Good Samaritan. It was so very close and Mr. Blanchard had meetings to attend today, so I thought I'd just come over and pay you a little visit. That way, I could give Olivia a report on how you are getting along —" She paused, her eyes narrowing in her plump, pink face.

"Oh, I'm just fine, thank you, Mrs. Blanchard," Toddy replied, still having some difficulty adjusting to the fact that Chris's mother had made a special trip to see her.

Mrs. Blanchard shifted her position slightly and settled her fur neckpiece a little before continuing.

"I'm very glad to hear that and to know that you are doing something useful with your life. One cannot expect handouts forever and I am sure it's a great burden removed from Olivia to have you on your own, especially now that dear Helene is gone."

At this, Toddy felt a rush of indignation. She checked the angry rebuttal that sprang to her lips. Hands clenched hotly behind her back, she managed to control an outburst. Surely this wasn't the reason Mrs. Blanchard had come? To go out of her way to be insulting?

Mrs. Blanchard moved uneasily. Toddy unconsciously braced herself as the woman cleared her throat.

"I *do* hope you will take this in the spirit intended, Toddy," she began tentatively, "but I did feel you ought to know Chris is back from South America. Poor dear, he looked dreadful when he returned home, so thin and sallow. He had a terrible bout with malaria while he was down there — anyway, he is much improved and has decided to go back to the University to get his engineering degree."

Pausing for breath, Mrs. Blanchard twisted the chain of her beaded handbag. "Of course, he had run off to those awful jungles after you so heartlessly . . . well, we needn't go into that, I suppose. But, I wanted you to understand that I feel — *we* feel, his father and I — that he is finally on the right track after his . . . disappointing setback. And . . . I hope . . . I do *sincerely* hope you will not try to contact him or to pick up any of the old destructive threads of your relationship with our son." Mrs. Blanchard's chins trembled in the fervor of her appeal. "What's past is past — Chris has a fine future ahead of him and I — *we* — feel any attempt on your part to —"

Toddy could not stand it a minute longer. She got to her feet and spoke in a voice she willed not to shake.

"Please, Mrs. Blanchard, there is no point in your saying any more. I understand you completely. Let me set your mind at ease. I have no intention of contacting Chris. As far as I'm concerned, he doesn't even know where I am, unless you've told him." Toddy swallowed hard. "I'm glad to hear he's doing well and that he's happy. Chris will always mean a great deal to me, but as far as attempting to disrupt his plans or his life —"

"Well, I wouldn't have put it so bluntly —" stammered Mrs. Blanchard, perhaps realizing she had gone too far.

"No? Well, how would you have put it, Mrs. Blanchard? You made yourself quite clear," Toddy replied coolly. Then checking her watch pinned to her apron, she said, "you will have to excuse me. I go on duty in ten minutes. Goodbye, Mrs. Blanchard, you may tell Mr. Blanchard you accomplished your mission."

Then Toddy turned and with all the dignity she could muster, she left the parlor and started up the stairs. But when she reached the landing the scalding tears spilled down her cheeks.

What Mrs. Blanchard said had hurt. But maybe she was right. About Mrs. Hale, about Chris.

"What's past is past." Chris was part of Toddy's past in Meadowridge. Now, more than ever, Toddy understood fully what she had always known. The Blanchards did not approve of her for their son. They never had accepted her and they never would. Any hope Toddy might have entertained about a future with Chris must be put away forever.

Yes, Mrs. Blanchard had achieved her end in coming. From now on, Toddy would banish everything else from her mind but her nurses' training.

22

1905–1906

Well into her second year Toddy found an almost immovable object on her way toward gaining her nursing certificate in the form of Miss Mabel Pryor, the supervisor of Student Nurses.

As they entered into this second year of training, the student nurses worked in pairs in the wards. Toddy was teamed with Helga Swenson, a sturdy, rosy-cheeked girl with flaxen braids from a Minnesota farm family. For all her robust appearance, Helga was terrified most of the time. She was afraid of Miss Pryor and all the head nurses, scared speechless around the doctors, nervous with the patients.

To offset her partner's paralyzing tension, Toddy joked, teased, did imitations of some of the more pompous members of the medical staff, particularly the overly important interns and residents.

One day when they were making beds together, one on each side, Toddy was at her most hilarious and Helga was giggling as they precisely turned neat corners and pulled the sheets tautly. Suddenly Miss Pryor's acid voice cracked behind them.

"There will be no levity on my ward, young ladies. Is that understood?"

Helga turned red then white and began shaking. Toddy immediately tried to straighten her face as they both chorused, "Yes, ma'am."

But as Miss Pryor turned and walked stiffly away, Toddy dissolved into helpless laughter and Helga pressed both hands against her mouth, her plump shoulders shaking with suppressed merriment.

Ever after that, at every opportunity, Toddy would come up to Helga and whisper sternly, "No levity!" and that was enough to send the poor girl into spasms of uncontrollable giggles.

Perhaps it was this ability not only to make others laugh but to laugh at herself that saw Toddy through some of the really hard and often sad times during her training.

Because she was naturally outgoing and friendly, Toddy was at her best with the patients. She seemed able to establish an instant rapport with them as she gave them a bath, brought food trays, or delivered medication. She always had a smile, a cheery greeting and listened to their complaints or worries with sympathetic attentiveness.

This was especially true with one patient, Mrs. Agnes O'Malley, an elderly woman who had been admitted for surgery. Because she was tiny and frail, the doctors wanted her to gain weight and strength before undergoing a scheduled operation.

During the time Toddy cared for her, she and Mrs. O'Malley formed a special relationship. The little lady was as optimistic and pleasant as Toddy, and they hit it off right away. The only thing she worried about while she was in the hospital, she confided to Toddy, was her two cats, her canary and her rosebushes.

"Mrs. Sutton, my neighbor, is taking care of Dickie, my bird, but the cats — you know they are such creatures of habit!" she said. "They like things to be the same. Eat out of the same little bowls in the same place in my kitchen by the stove, and they like their cream a little warm — you know how 'tis?"

Toddy nodded as she gently smoothed the sheets and turned the pillowcase.

"And pretty soon my rosebushes will need pruning and who's to see to that?"

As the day for Mrs. O'Malley's surgery drew near, she fretted more. "I do hope as soon as my operation's over the doctors will let me go home pretty quick. I don't like to be away from my little family any longer than necessary. They depend on me so."

From chatting with Mrs. O'Malley every day, Toddy got a mental picture of her small cosy house, of the two cats and the bright yellow canary in its cage in the window of her snug little kitchen, "singing his tiny heart out" as Mrs. O'Malley was fond of remarking. It was Toddy who prepared her when the day of her surgery came, and it was she who walked alongside the guerney, holding her hand as they wheeled her down the corridor to the operating room.

"I'll be here when you wake up, Mrs. O'Malley," she promised the old lady as she left her at the door of OR.

But when Toddy came back on duty, she noticed Mrs. O'Malley's bed had been stripped. Hurrying over to the rack of charts, Toddy pulled Mrs. O'Malley's and found it marked PATIENT DECEASED. A sob escaped Toddy and she put her head down on the counter and wept.

Fingers pressed hard into her shoulder and a sharp voice hissed into her ear, "Miss Todd, come into my office at once." Hastily Toddy straightened up, replaced the chart, and followed the rigid figure of the head nurse into her office. There Miss Pryor confronted her severely.

"Miss Todd, the cardinal rule of nursing is not to become emotionally involved with the patients. You give them the best care you are capable of, but you do not let yourself be drawn into their personal lives. If you do, you will fail as a nurse, fail the very patients who need you. Is that clearly understood? Now get back on the ward, there is work to be done."

Toddy bit back angry words, checked the indignant tears. What about Mrs. O'Malley's poor little kitties? Her bird? Her roses? What would become of her things? She was alone in the world, she had told Toddy, after years of working as a housekeeper to a family in San Francisco. She had bought her little house with her savings when she retired.

Now, Toddy was supposed to forget all about her?

During the next few months Toddy was tried to the very limits. No one saw the enormous effort it took for her to accept correction, reprimand, a misunderstood explanation, a mistaken or unwarranted scolding from a head matron. No one ever saw the tears wept into her pillow late at night, the overwhelming feeling of exhaustion, of desperate longing to escape the inflexible routine.

She had packed Helene's worn New Testament in her trunk when she left to come away to Nursing School and nightly Toddy sought the solace and strength she needed. She missed Helene's soft voice reading aloud as she used to, but the remarkable thing, it seemed to Toddy, was how often the verse or Scripture she turned to was exactly the right one for that moment of need. It was almost as if Helene had become her guardian angel watching over her, caring for her during those long months.

And then, at the end of the year of training, Toddy had a long-overdue opportunity to rest, to spend two weeks in Meadowridge. Because she had wanted to be sure Toddy could be there, Mrs. Hale had waited until this time to plan a special event.

In her will, Helene had left money for a very specific project, one that had occupied her grandmother for the past year and a half — a bequest for a Children's Room to be added to the Meadowridge Library. The dedication was to take place during Toddy's vacation.

Helene had been very specific about the addition. "It should have lots of windows so it is full of sunlight," she had stated. "And there should be low shelves filled with books so that the children can reach them, little round tables and small chairs so they can sit down and look at the books to decide which ones they want to take home."

The bequest was so like Helene, Toddy thought, a perfect "memorial" to a young woman who had loved books and reading and who had, herself, always been a child at heart.

As Toddy boarded the train in St. Louis to make the trip to Meadowridge, she was strongly reminded of the "Orphan Train" that had first taken her to Meadowridge and into the Hale home. Thoughts of the bleak days at Greystone, of her friends Laurel and Kit, of Mrs. Scott and that long, "scary" trip over the mountains and along the prairies, carrying them to an unknown destiny were vivid.

Along with the memories came the childhood doubts and uncertainties she had usually managed to mask behind activity and hard work and a bright smile. Still, lurking in her heart of hearts was the question, *Is there any place I really belong?*

Almost before she was ready, Toddy heard the conductor calling out the next stop.

"Meadowridge! Next stop, Meadowridge!"

She had not sent word of the exact time of her arrival, so there was no one to meet her at the station. It was better this way, actually, for Toddy had a sense of melancholy as she remembered the last time she had stood on this platform. Helene had been with her then. They had been leaving for their grand tour to Europe and were full of hopes and plans. Now, she was back here alone.

She left her suitcase to be delivered to the house later, and taking only one small valise, began walking along the familiar streets from the train station, then turned up the hill toward the Hale house.

At the gate she paused, struggling with her emotions, imagining Helene's face at an upstairs window, waving to her as she had done so often. Toddy stood there, her hand on the latch for a moment, before she pushed it open and started up the walk to the veranda.

But before she reached the first step, the front door opened and Mrs. Hale came out. She held out both arms and Toddy dropped her valise and ran up the steps and into Olivia's embrace.

"Oh, Toddy, I'm so glad you're here!" Olivia's voice broke. "Welcome home, my dear girl."

Toddy leaned her head on Olivia's

shoulder, sobbing, knowing for the first time in her life, without any doubt, that she had come home at last.

The day of the dedication was very warm. The noon ceremony was to take place in the main library at the doorway into the Children's Room. In attendance were the Mayor, members of the City Council, the ministers from all four Meadowridge churches, each to give a short invocation or benediction. Following the speeches and the ribbon cutting, the ladies belonging to the local "Friends of the Library" were to hold a reception out on the side yard and lawn of the library. The event had been given front-page coverage in the *Meadowridge Monitor* and many more townspeople than held library cards came thronging in to witness the proceedings.

As the sun outside climbed into its midday position, the crowded library grew very hot. By the time all the speeches were given, many were anxious to get out into the cooler air and quench their thirst with the gallons of lemonade provided by the Refreshment Committee.

People immediately surrounded Mrs. Hale to shake her hand and to add their personal appreciation for this wonderful gift to the community left by her granddaughter. The first crush of well-wishers seemed to startle Olivia a little and as she took a few steps back, Toddy stepped protectively to her side. One of the ladies quickly organized a more orderly receiving line for people to express their thanks.

Looking down the line Toddy saw, to her dismay, Bernice Blanchard! Toddy had not seen Chris's mother since that fatal day at Good Samaritan. Still, she was bound to run into the woman sometime during her stay in Meadowridge and she tensed, trying to prepare herself for what could not help but be an uncomfortable encounter. Fervently praying that by the time Mrs. Blanchard reached her, she would be able to handle it graciously, Toddy attempted to focus only on the next person in line.

Despite her distraction Toddy heard Mrs. Hale saying something quite astonishing.

"Have you met my *other* granddaughter, Toddy?" Mrs. Hale was saying.

Toddy wasn't even sure that she had heard correctly until Mrs. Hale repeated the same phrase several times in the course of the next few introductions. It was particularly gratifying that she said it clearly to the couple right in front of Mrs. Blanchard, and

Toddy could not help deriving some secret satisfaction in seeing Mrs. B's reaction. She seemed quite flushed and flustered as she reached them.

"A lovely occasion, Olivia," Mrs. Blanchard mumbled, holding out a limp hand as Mrs. Hale acknowledged her comment and passed her on toward Toddy.

But at that very moment, Mrs. Blanchard's face became very red then just as quickly blanched. Her eyes rolled back and she began to slump, her knees buckling, until she fell onto the grass.

There was a gasp from the bystanders who stood staring dumbly down at the prone figure as if struck into stone statues. Toddy sprang into action.

"Get back, everyone, give her air!" she said in a commanding tone.

In a moment, she was kneeling beside Mrs. Blanchard, loosening the buttons on the side of her high lace collar, freeing her throat. Then slipping one arm under her shoulders, she raised the woman slightly and with her other free hand she removed the stiff, straw picture hat.

"Someone, soak some napkins with ice water and bring them to me," Toddy ordered and someone scurried to obey.

Mrs. Blanchard's hair had come out of its

pins and fell forward over her face. Toddy held her firmly as she unhooked the tight sash around Mrs. Blanchard's plump waist. As some dripping napkins were thrust at her, Toddy snapped, "Squeeze out the water." When this was done, she took one and pressed it against the back of Mrs. Blanchard's bare neck. The other she held against the woman's forehead.

In the meantime, others recognizing Toddy was in charge had managed to keep the people back, leaving a wide ring of gawkers around the stricken woman so that air could circulate.

Soon, a low moan escaped from Mrs. Blanchard's pale lips and her eyelids began to flutter slightly. At the same time, someone came pushing through the crowd. It was a perspiring Mr. Blanchard, wiping his bald head in agitation. Evidently someone had run over to the bank to tell him his wife had collapsed.

As soon as she saw her husband, Bernice began to whimper. He bent over her.

"It's all right, old dearie. I'm here now. We'll get you home. You're going to be fine —" his voice trailed off anxiously and he looked over at Toddy for reassurance.

"I'll come with you," she said firmly.

With her help, Mr. Blanchard got his wife

to her feet and as she leaned against him, Toddy went to support her on the other side. Together they walked her slowly inside the library.

The crowd made a path for Dr. Woodward who had attended the dedication and ceremony. He had sent someone for his medical bag and was hurrying to assist them.

"Good work." He nodded to Toddy as he and Mr. Blanchard helped Bernice to sit down.

"I'll go get the buggy, my dear," Mr. Blanchard told her.

For the first time that anyone could remember, Mrs. Blanchard failed to instruct her husband in how to do whatever it was he planned to do. She sat there weakly, propped up in the chair, looking wan and pale. She made no protest as Toddy kept the folded damp napkin pressed against the back of her neck, the other on her forehead.

By the time Mr. Blanchard was back, Dr. Woodward assured them both that Bernice had not suffered a heart attack but had simply been overcome by the heat, the sun and the excitement. She would be fine after a day's rest in bed, drinking plenty of liquids.

"I suggest, however, that Toddy go up to

the house with you," he said.

Mr. Blanchard looked grateful at the suggestion.

At the Blanchard's house a frightened Annie came upstairs with them and scurried ahead to turn down Bernice's bed. Toddy helped her get Bernice into her nightgown and into bed.

Before she closed her eyes wearily, Bernice reached out and took Toddy's hand in her clammy one.

"Thank you, dear," she whispered weakly. "No matter what Lee Woodward says, I know you saved my life."

Toddy did not argue. She knew, of course, that Dr. Woodward's diagnosis of a slight sunstroke was correct. But what was important was that the animosity she had always felt from Bernice Blanchard had disappeared. In today's incident Toddy had found an unexpected place to belong — in the heart of Chris's mother.

23

Then almost before it seemed possible, the three years had come to an end, and it was time for the State examinations. Now was the ultimate test of whether Toddy would qualify to reach her goal. The exams would cover everything she was supposed to have assimilated, would test her intelligence, her memory, the daily practice of the nursing skills she had acquired.

The three days of exams, two a day, morning and afternoon, left Toddy drained. The third day Toddy and some of the classmates with whom she had struggled and worked and shared in such close companionship throughout their training, went out for dinner to a favorite Italian restaurant to celebrate. Or at least try to forget for a few hours that the State Examiners were deciding their combined fates.

A week later when the news circulated throughout the school that the exam grades were posted, Toddy was among the first scrambling down the steps into the front hall to search the list on the bulletin board for her name. She did not have to look long or far. ZEPHRONIA VICTORINE TODD was at the top of the graduating class.

Graduation date was scheduled and invitations to family and friends sent out. Mrs. Hale was coming.

Unlike many of her fellow nurses who had applied to hospitals near their hometowns, Toddy had not thought much further than Graduation Day itself. So she was surprised when Miss Pryor called her into her office and encouraged her to apply for a position right there at Good Samaritan.

"All your teachers and supervisors have given you excellent recommendations, Todd. You have the combination of nursing skills and the right attitude to make an outstanding nurse. I have watched your progress carefully and have noted that you have conquered your original tendencies to be too personally concerned with your patients. Nurses deal with life and death every day and unless you want to be broken by it, you must discipline yourself and cultivate the needed professionalism to withstand the emotional strain."

Toddy was both pleased and gratified by her supervisor's compliment. Still, Toddy was unsure. She felt she needed a stronger leading before she made a commitment about her future. Besides there was something still in her own mind she needed to settle.

Leaving Miss Pryor's office, Toddy went into the chapel and sat there quietly. Late afternoon sunlight streamed through the stained-glass window over the altar, illuminating the picture of the Good Samaritan tending the wounds of the injured traveler. Underneath was the inscription: ". . . Inasmuch as ye have done it unto one of the least of these my brethren, ye have done it unto me" (Matthew 25:40).

Where would the Lord have her serve? Toddy asked herself. How could she find guidance for where to go to best use her nursing skills, these years of training? In time, God would show her the way. She could trust Him for that.

As she came out of the chapel, she met two of her friends just coming in.

One of them smiled and whispered, "You've got company waiting for you in the parlor, Toddy."

She wondered if Mrs. Hale had arrived early for graduation. Toddy had made reservations for her in one of the nicest hotels in town, but had not expected her until the next afternoon. She hurried to the visitor's parlor. At the doorway she stopped short.

Instead of Mrs. Hale, a tall young man

rose to his feet at her entrance.

"Chris!" Toddy gasped.

"Hello, Toddy."

It had been almost four years and as Toddy's eyes widened in astonishment, she saw how much he had changed. The lanky leanness of boyhood had become a broad-shouldered manliness, the boyishly handsome features now strongly molded in a deeply tanned face.

"Oh, Chris, how wonderful to see you!" exclaimed Toddy, holding out both hands to him. "How did you know I was here?"

Chris put down the bouquet of pink and white carnations he was holding to take Toddy's extended hands in a tight grip.

"My mother!" He grinned. "When I got home last fall, she told me all about how you'd saved her life!"

"Nonsense! I didn't, of course." Toddy smiled. "But I'm so glad to see you. Please sit down." She gestured to a chair. "There's so much to catch up on, so much I want to know about you, Chris."

"Well, I went back to the University and got my degree and was back in Meadowridge for a few weeks before starting a new job in Arizona. I went by to see Mrs. Hale and she told me all about you — says you're graduating at the top of your class. Congratulations, Toddy. I'm proud of you." Then he looked at her and, grinning his old boyish grin, asked, "May I come to your graduation?"

Toddy felt her heart turn over.

"Of course you may! Chris, I can hardly believe you're really here!"

"Well, I wasn't sure you'd see me." Grinning, he ducked his head in a familiar shy gesture. Then, he said, "Mrs. Hale's been traveling every time I've been home, it seems, the house closed. I didn't even hear about Helene until —" he halted, then said sympathetically, "I'm so sorry, Toddy, I know how much she meant to you,"

"Yes, thank you, Chris," Toddy replied. "Actually that's why I'm in nursing. I want to spend my life helping other people like Helene —" she halted, blushing. "I hope that doesn't sound pretentious, for goodness sake!" She rolled her eyes.

Chris reached over and covered her hand with his big, rough one.

"Not at all. It sounds like the Toddy I know, impulsive, generous —" He paused a moment before adding, "It sounds like the Toddy I *love*."

Toddy looked into the eyes regarding her with such tenderness and drew in her breath.

"I *do* love you, Toddy, you know that,

don't you? I always have and I always will."
Chris rushed on, "The main reason I came
up here to see you now is because I wanted
to tell you that. I've not changed about that.
I never will. There's never been anyone else
for me, Toddy."

"Oh, Chris, don't say any more. Not now.
Not yet."

"Then *when*, Toddy? Will there be a time
you'll listen to what I have to say, what's
been in my heart all these years?"

She nodded. "Yes, Chris, perhaps. But
not right now. I have tomorrow to think
about and —"

"After tomorrow?" he persisted.

Toddy got to her feet, holding the bouquet like a shield in front of her. "Chris, I
have to go. There's a Graduation rehearsal
in twenty minutes." He rose too, towering
over her.

"All right, Toddy. I can wait. I've waited
this long." He smiled ruefully. "I'll see you
tomorrow then."

"Yes, Chris, tomorrow," Toddy promised.

The organ music of the Processional re-
verberated into the arched nave of the hospital chapel as the twenty nursing students
marched in solemnly and took their places

in the two front pews.

The distinguished looking Chief-of-Staff, Dr. Willoughby, stood at the podium with Miss Pryor at his side. As each young woman's name was called, she mounted the altar steps and received her rolled and ribboned certificate. Miss Pryor pinned her RN pin onto the collar of her stiffly starched new white uniform. There was, as they say, hardly a dry eye among those attending the ceremony.

When Toddy's turn came, Olivia Hale unashamedly wiped her eyes, watching as the petite, slim figure in white, the newly earned fluted organdy cap perched on her shining red-gold hair, accepted her hard-earned reward.

After Dr. Willoughby congratulated them, Miss Pryor took her place at the podium and spoke directly to the new nurses.

"Perhaps only those of us who have come along the same path can fully appreciate and understand what your cap, pin and certificate mean. *I do know* and it is with heartfelt sincerity that I commend each of you on this important day of your lives.

"What you have shown and will continue to show in this vocation you have chosen is a deep respect for life. We here at Good Samaritan have tried to instill in you that respect.

"What does it mean? It means that every life has value, no matter how new, no matter how old, no matter how rich, no matter how poor. It means that every human being is treated with dignity, no matter how sick, no matter how weak, no matter how wretched, no matter how lost.

"It means that every person is a gift from God, no matter what religion, no matter what color, no matter what age, no matter what nationality.

"This is our creed, our calling. We have tried to pass this on to you young women as you start your nursing careers, so that you might give to the world this same devotion, that your lives may be lived for the honor and glory of God."

When the benediction was pronounced, Toddy rose with the first row of nurses and moved out into the aisle for the Recessional. Through eyes misted with happy tears, she searched out one face among all the others in the crowded sanctuary.

There at the back as she passed. Chris! He had come, and suddenly their future seemed possible.

24

1908

Spring came to Meadowridge late but then seemed to explode. Blossoming orchards scented the air with rare perfume, every garden gone crazy with color. The May of which poets rhapsodized became reality.

On just such a morning in the second week of May, up on the hill at the Hales', the household was stirring early, busy with preparations for the noon wedding.

It was a wedding that no one had been sure would ever take place. Certainly not Bernice Blanchard, who was at the moment trying to decide between two hats most appropriate for the "mother of the groom," albeit a reluctant one. She had thought her opposition and their long separation would have broken the strong link between the two young people.

For that matter, Olivia Hale had had her own reservations about the match. Surely these two strong personalities would continue to clash as they had in childhood, with foolish quarrels, disagreements and disputes. Their backgrounds and experiences had given them different perspectives, formed new attitudes. Could basic incompatibility of temperament and character be bridged as adults?

Toddy herself, not denying the strong mutual attraction she and Chris had always been aware of since high school, recognized some of the problems of their relationship. She had not been as easily convinced as Chris that they were "meant for each other."

She pored over the Scriptures she had learned to search out for life's big decisions, studying any reference to choosing a mate or marrying. The one that concerned her was from the third chapter of Amos: "Can two walk together except they be agreed?" Were she and Chris enough alike to spend the rest of their lives together? Or on the other hand, too much alike? Impulsive, quick-tempered, strong-willed?

When Chris persisted, Toddy begged for more time.

But in the two years since graduating from nurse's training, much had happened to draw them closer, to help them understand each other better, to recognize the other's good qualities, accept the differences, share each other's hopes and dreams.

Most of all to learn to love each other in a new and deeper way that was both binding and freeing.

At Mrs. Hale's suggestion Toddy had come back with her to Meadowridge. She had found it difficult not to burst into tears when Mrs. Hale extended the invitation. She was wanted! She belonged! And when she arrived, Clara was there to greet her, too. "Welcome home, Toddy!"

Chris left reluctantly for his job in Arizona, but persisted in his suit by letter and as many frequent trips to Meadowridge as he could manage.

Observing Mrs. Hale, into her seventies now, Toddy saw that she was slowing down. Her eyesight was failing and, when fall came, Toddy was loath to leave her. So when Dr. Woodward offered her a job as his office nurse three days a week, Toddy accepted. She also registered herself to be on call if needed at the new Community Hospital.

It had been a good year, a worthwhile, productive year. More and more Toddy felt her special place in Olivia's heart becoming firmly established. It was a place which belonged to no one else, a place she had earned. She knew she had found her niche in nursing as well, and she felt at peace that she was doing God's will for her life.

Then Chris came to tell her he had been put in charge of the entire project in Arizona, beginning the first of the year, and he wanted Toddy to come back with him. She knew she could delay her answer no longer and went to Mrs. Hale, sharing all her own thoughts, her feelings, her questions.

Mrs. Hale leaned forward and took Toddy's face in both her hands. "My dear girl, you have given me so much. I could never repay you for all the happiness you have brought into my life and, of course, Helene's. Now it is your time. Go with a free heart and mind. A fine young man loves you. Take the life he is offering you and be grateful for such a love. You have my blessing."

So on this beautiful May morning Toddy finished her final packing. After the ceremony she and Chris would leave for Arizona, going straight to the train station from the reception Mrs. Blanchard insisted on giving them.

Toddy was both calm and excited. The only shadow on this lovely day was that Helene was not here to share it with her. In the garden, as Toddy gathered lilacs, pink tulips, grape hyacinths and lily of the valley for her wedding bouquet, Helene was much in her thoughts. Helene had loved flowers and these were among her favorites.

Toddy had not wanted a big, elaborate wedding and had stood quietly determined against all Mrs. Blanchard's pleas about the "social obligations" she and Chris's father needed to fulfill.

"It's *our* wedding, Mrs. Blanchard," Toddy reminded her firmly. "And we just want the people *we* love and care about to celebrate with us when we marry."

Chris, too, was adamant and so Bernice gave in with a sigh of resignation.

But as she sat beside her husband, wearing the elegant chapeau she had finally decided upon, in the Meadowridge Church filled with Toddy and Chris's high-school friends, Bernice had to admit that the ceremony was perfect. The bridegroom, of course, was quite the handsomest and even the bride, in her simple cream boucle traveling suit, lace blouse and biscuit straw hat, looked dainty and attractive.

As Toddy left the church on Chris's arm, she whispered, "Before we leave for the reception, there is something I want to do."

Hand in hand they walked together up the hill to the church cemetery. Inside, Toddy quickly found what she was looking for — a headstone engraved:

HELENE ELIZABETH HALE
1879–1902

Beneath the inscription Toddy herself had chosen, "The Redeemed of the Lamb," was a favorite verse of Scripture: "And God shall wipe away all tears from their eyes; and there shall be no more death, neither sorrow, nor crying, neither shall there be any more pain . . ." (Revelation 21:4).

Chris thoughtfully took a few steps back, leaving Toddy standing alone in quiet contemplation beside Helene's grave.

Then she knelt and placed her bridal bouquet at the headstone. As she did so, she felt a release of the one sad little corner of her heart that had so deeply missed her beloved sister this day. After a few more minutes, Toddy rose and held out her hand to Chris.

He came forward, tucked Toddy's small hand into his arm and together they strode out through the gate and into the new life they had waited so long to begin together.